DAWNS
A NEW DAY

Other titles by
Danielle Ackley-McPhail

THE ETERNAL CYCLE SERIES
Yesterday's Dreams
Tomorrow's Memories
Today's Promise

THE ETERNAL WANDERINGS SERIES
Eternal Wanderings

THE BAD-ASS FAERIE TALE SERIES
The Halfling's Court
The Redcap's Queen
The High King's Fool
(forthcoming)

Baba Ali and the Clockwork Djinn
(with Day Al-Mohamed)

The Literary Handyman
Build-A-Book Workshop
More Tips From the Handyman

The Ginger KICK! Cookbook

SHORT FICTION
A Legacy of Stars
Transcendence
Consigned to the Sea
Flash in the Can
The Fox's Fire
The Kindly One
The Die Is Cast
(with Mike McPhail)

DAWNS
A NEW DAY
AND OTHER FUTURISTIC TALES

Danielle Ackley-McPhail

PAPER PHOENIX PRESS

Pennsville, NJ

PUBLISHED BY
Paper Phoenix Press
A division of eSpec Books
PO Box 242
Pennsville, NJ 08070
www.especbooks.com

ISBN: 978-1-949691-77-1
ISBN (ebook): 978-1-949691-76-4

"Dawns a New Day" previously published in *Footprints in the Stars*, edited by Danielle Ackley-McPhail, published by eSpec Books.
"The Steady Drone of Silence" previously published in *If We Had Known*, edited by Mike McPhail, published by eSpec Books.
"Travellin' Show" previously published in *Space Tramps*, edited by Jennifer Brozek, published by Flying Pen Press.
"Casualties of War" previously published in *Man and Machine*, edited by Mike McPhail, published by eSpec Books.
"The Devil's Own Luck" previously published in *Lucky 13*, edited by John L. French, published by Padwolf Publishing.
 "No Man Left Behind" previously published in *In Harm's Way*, edited by Mike McPhail, published by eSpec Books.
"New Discoveries" previously published in *Stories of Fremont's Children*, edited by Brenda Cooper and Danielle Ackley-McPhail, published by eSpec Books.

Cover Art: sci-fi concept of the man with robotic arm standing on ruined buildings looking at sunset sky with digital art style, illustration painting © By Tithi Luadthong, www.shutterstock.com
Cover Design: Mike McPhail, McP Digital Graphics
Interior Design: Danielle McPhail
Copyediting: Greg Schauer

DEDICATION

To those that come after,
learn from our mistakes,
not our examples.

Contents

DAWNS A NEW DAY

*"I get knocked down, but I get up again.
You're never gonna keep me down." – Chumbawamba*

CHARLIE DIDN'T KNOW WHERE THEY CAME FROM. WHAT THEY WERE. All that mattered was that her momma had held them dear. There were so many memories of her raising her hands mere inches from the plastic-wrapped mounds of boxes, her expression filled with awe and fear and longing in equal measure. Beneath those, the barest flicker of hope, all but extinguished.

These were remnants from a past Charlie had never seen. Never touched. No one had touched them. That was the point. The thing that made them so precious.

Part of her longed for these things. To open and explore those boxes and all they contained, driven by an insatiable curiosity. Part of her remained indifferent, not understanding the significance of those untouched objects. How could she? Charlie had never been a part of that world, the one that existed before *it* was found.

*From the journal of
Amelia Gates,
Forensic Technologist,
Circa 1 N.A.*

The artifact was discovered in a pile of cooling rock at the edge of a new fissure vent on Mount Vesuvius. Markings covered the sleek tooled-metal sides, vaguely familiar, as if we <u>should</u> know them, but unlike any identifiable form of writing ever studied since the beginning of recorded history. Smooth and ageless. A timeless *work of art. Clearly manufactured but by no means anyone recognized, of materials that defy identification. The object evoked a sense of wonder in all who saw it, followed by the overwhelming desire to discover its secrets. Some said it glowed faintly green outside of direct light. They craved to touch it. Others couldn't get away quick enough. To the media, it was pure gold... even though it wasn't.*

They lived in a library. At a college where Momma had sometimes taught in the before time. Not out in the open, where anyone could see them through the plate-glass windows, but in a back room—Momma called it a break room—with no windows at all. But at night... from a young age, Charlie had roamed the stacks by moonlight devouring any book she could reach. The words on the page fascinated her nearly as much as Momma's boxes. Agriculture. Science. Modern Dance. Computer Programming. Cooking. Herblore. Mathematics. Any and all knowledge drew her interest.

She explored her little world, imagining what it was like full of people doing and working on things she'd only read about. She sat at the computers and pretended they were still full of light and life and knowledge. But never when Momma might catch her.

Sometimes for hours she would sit there and turn them on and off just to watch the screen glow to life, powered by the solar panels they'd installed on the roof.

From the journal of
Amelia Gates,
Forensic Technologist,
Circa 2.3 N.A.

They didn't bomb us into the Stone Age—whoever they are... or were—but they did set us on our collective technological asses. It took us a little while to figure out what was going on. The virus spread over time, slow but steady. Unrealized and insidious. We don't even understand how it happened. How it could happen. The damage already irreparable before we even figured out what was going on. Like any social disease, by the time someone determined how it spread the damage was done. In less than six months one hundred years of computer development began to unravel.

You would have thought the first systems affected would be those in direct contact with the artifact, but they weren't. The world had begun to deteriorate even before the object hit the testing phase. We were doomed the moment it was found. *The moment the kid who fell over it picked it up in awe to marvel at his find. No one bothered with quarantine procedures. It was a thing brought up from the earth, purified by fire. Who would have thought we needed to?*

At first innocuous things—like ATMs and health trackers and home PCs—glitched, then seemed to be fine. Until they weren't. Driving any car built after 1968 carried an element of risk in proportion to the number of computer chips that went into its design and their respective functions. People fell back on the old ways. Thrift stores and consignment shops and junkyards became the new places to shop. Anywhere people could find old tech. The type anyone could repair. Things that didn't need a computer degree to operate.

The attack was multipronged, we determined that much.

Things couldn't fail all at once. That would be self-limiting. Our dependency had to persist for the contagion to spread. Anything mankind touched became a carrier until every computerized system melted away like so much broken code.

Not all of our tech failed. Just anything with roots set in Silicon Valley. Like a person with dementia, the hardware worked just fine; the software... that shredded like books torn page from page. *Anything networked followed. Corporate. Government. Military. International. It didn't matter. No system was safe. Not even those beyond Earth's sphere. We didn't learn that until satellites started falling from the sky. And who knows what happened to the ISS.*

Our technological base crumbled as exponentially as it had grown. No one knew how to cope, knocked back into a strictly mechanical world.

Charlie had always been told never to touch the things in Momma's prohibited stash, but they called to her. Captured her attention and would not let go. They were smooth and bright and looked cool to the touch. She resisted the call for a while, but couldn't manage forever.

Once, when Momma was away finding food, Charlie crept close and pulled one of the objects from its cocoon. It was flat, like one of the handheld chalkboards she'd learned her words on, but when she touched a depression on the side bright light came from beneath the center glass. A mere touch called up pictures that moved, colorful and cute, like it was meant for a child. She was lost in the glow and the movement, hardly noticing Momma's return.

She had looked up from the tablet to see a look of horror on her mother's face. Charlie quickly dropped her gaze and thrust the forbidden object away from her. She watched Momma through her lashes as Momma snatched it up and the shock turned to awe as she swiped a finger across the screen. Within ten minutes the pictures had stuttered and gone dark, but Charlie would never forget the awe in Momma's expression or how the ever-present flicker of hope had fanned higher.

Momma had dropped the dead tablet and scooped Charlie up in a tight hug, murmuring, "Could it be that simple?" Charlie hadn't known what she meant. Then.

She remembered growing tenser as the seconds passed, her nerves on overload until she had stiffly jerked away, avoiding her mother's fleeting look of hurt as she bobbed back and forth until the stress bled away.

"Don't worry, my special child," Momma had murmured. "I understand."

Momma has been gone a while now, the life gone out of her, just like the computers out in the library. Only there was no way to turn her on and off again. All Charlie had left of her was her journal, the pages soft and creased and worn with rereading, still echoing with Momma's voice.

Charlie used the knowledge she'd gained from it to carry on.

*From the journal of
Amelia Gates,
Forensic Technologist,
Circa 4 N.A.*

We tried to rebuild and that is when the truth came out. It wasn't just the computer systems that had been scrambled. The virus messed with our minds, rewrote our DNA and jumbled our thought processes until anything related to computer tech read like ancient Greek.

Going off the grid was no longer a matter of choice. The preppers had a field day being right. Everyone else clambered to catch up. Alternate energy sources kept the lights on, so to speak. Factories reworked their high-tech processes and dusted off mothballed machines from a bygone age. Craftsmen of any type were once more shown respect. It wasn't enough to save us.

As a society we became brutal. Grabbing for whatever we needed. Grabbing for what we could keep. Instead of working together to rebuild, most of us went to ground, afraid of the ensuing chaos. Some helped their fellow man... as much as they were able... but the new normal terrified us.

Individually, we are capable of being noble. But humanity as a whole is horrifying when it's afraid. We could have sustained society quite well on low-tech, as we had for most of our existence, if not for our fear. Unwittingly, we destroyed technology. Knowingly, we destroyed ourselves.

It was time to remove the plastic. Time to open the boxes. It was time to honor the legacy Momma had left her because without that legacy, there was no way to rebuild. For a fleeting moment, Charlie bobbed in agitation. The stricture against touching these things firmly ingrained. But the inner conflict could not stand against her overwhelming desire to discover the mysteries those boxes held.

First, she moved everything from the room in which she had lived for fifteen years, all but Momma's stash, the large, battered linoleum table, and a single chair. Then she cleaned the space until not even a speck of dust remained, then cleaned it again. The linoleum was well beyond shining, but it did gleam.

And then she stared at Momma's legacy. Large boxes and small, the word "Gateway" emblazoned along the sides. Fitting, even if Charlie had no idea why that word was chosen. With meticulous care, she opened each one, drew out its hidden treasure, and set the box aside, careful to group the contents with the papers for each component. Monitors. Keyboards. Towers. Mice. Laptops. Tablets. Five of each, except the tablets. All untouched until now. All uninfected. Once destined to teach the next generation. Now destined to save it.

A small foundation upon which to rebuild the world.

Challenge accepted.

Without even unwrapping the manuals, Charlie set up her empire. Wires neat and orderly, components correctly and precisely placed, power source engaged. She reached for the power button, then slowly drew her hand away. Momma's written words came back to her: *the hardware worked just fine; the software... that shredded like books torn page from page.*

Alone in this back room, touched only by her hand, these computers were fine. But no matter what she did here, it would never be enough. She had to rebuild. She had to reconnect. The infrastructure was out there, blank and void and waiting, but she never could dare touch it running on the old code. She needed to rewrite the language... she needed an anti-virus.

Pushing away from the table, she went for a walk, her mind working furiously on the problem. For days, then weeks Charlie went on many walks...

From the journal of
Amelia Gates,
Forensic Technologist,
Circa 5 N.A.

–The final entry–

Society shattered like a finely balanced glass globe knocked from its plinth. Have the past five years been our crucible? Will the shards of society be reformed better or worse than what we had been? Right now all I see is a dark time, but I have begun to expect not everyone has been affected by the virus. That those on the spectrum, like my Charlie, are wired different enough to remain unaffected.

Is this our light in the darkness? I look at my daughter and wonder...

Charlie sat back hard on her heels and tracing the webbing of scars across the back of her hand to restore order to her own mind. Agitated, she resisted the urge to flutter that hand just as much as she resisted the urge to reach out and run her fingers through the pile of shards before her, looking for order in the chaos, her mind already fast at work on putting that meaningless puzzle together, no matter how pointless it might seem.

She watched the play of light and shadow on the dusty fragments, hinting at their former brilliance. The refraction of the images captured in the larger fragments. Her gaze narrowed and her hands twitched, her head going completely still as her mind dove into the enigma, followed by her hands, sorting bits of glass with short, sharp motions, heedless of the specks of blood left behind on them. Her hands sorted glass, but her mind sorted facts. So many facts stored away over what had to be over a decade of reading the scholarly treasure trove that filled her home. She was almost there this time. Nearly broken through...

Abruptly, she drew her hands back, her motions rigidly controlled as she rose to her feet and hurried to her hidden warren, seeking out the blank pages at the back of Amelia Gates' journal. Back to the pristine monitor and tower she'd dared not touch, unwrapped from its plastic and patiently waiting for the dawning of a new day. The dawning of a new way.

It was here. She had it. The start of a new way of thinking. A way out of the darkness. A way back up to the stars. And Momma so help her, when she got there, she was going to make the race responsible pay.

The Steady Drone of Silence

"Excuse me? Lieutenant Kolby... excuse me!" Christopher James spoke softly into the headset attached to the helmet the lieutenant had jammed onto his head before they'd left the transport. "I need to know what's gone wrong..."

Just ahead, Kolby snapped around to look over his shoulder, his features hard-set and his gaze unyielding. His posture projected urgency.

Christopher fell silent as he felt his eyes widen and the rest of him go cold. *This must be how a rabbit feels caught in a hawk's sights,* he thought as he swallowed hard and fought the urge to duck his head. Kolby looked away and continued his hurried, but methodical progress through the brush, his eyes continually scanning in all directions, even straight up into the sky.

A shiver ran over Christopher. *Why would the lieutenant look up?*

Clutching the straps of the rucksack holding his tablet computer, he did his best to move as quickly and quietly as the soldiers escorting him. Fat chance of that, though. He was a civilian contractor. An engineer. A tech head specializing in unmanned aerial vehicles, or UAVs. Two weeks ago he'd been pulled from his current research project with no explanation. Now he found himself on the butt end of Demeter traipsing through the wilds, destination unknown. He didn't have to ask to know the soldiers escorting him weren't any happier about it than he was.

Maybe he should have been paying more attention to where he was walking, instead of worrying over where he was going. Abruptly, his forward motion switched to downward as a root or something snagged his foot, tripping him. Christopher started to cry out only to find himself gripped by what felt like two steel bands, one across his mouth, the other around his upper arm. He had the vague impression the rest of the soldiers around him had dropped low to the ground and gone still. Christopher himself couldn't help but tremble as he came eye to up-close eye with Lieutenant Kolby.

"Do you *want* to die?" The words were so low and emphatic Christopher questioned if he'd actually heard them, either way the message was clear in Kolby's gaze.

Christopher shook his head.

Kolby looked over at the soldier to their left. Samson, if Christopher remembered correctly. Hanging from the man's neck was an electronic device. Some kind of tracker-slash-monitor. All Christopher knew was the little green light on the top of the housing meant they were good. If the red one went on, they were screwed. The man nodded and Kolby nodded back. Only then did he release his grip on Christopher. One hand dropped to the rifle hanging from the strap slung across Kolby's chest, the other rose slowly into the air in an obscure gesture Christopher had to guess meant 'proceed', because—as if they were guided by one brain—the six soldiers rose from where they crouched and continued through the brush with barely a sound.

Christopher couldn't move.

The soldier behind him gave him a controlled shove. Not enough to make him fall, but enough to break the grip of the fear anchoring Christopher in place. He was terrified of messing up again. He was terrified of whatever was out there that had Kolby treading so lightly. He was terrified of never making it home.

Christopher had no place being on this mission.

Apparently the military felt otherwise. Or at least someone up the chain of command did.

Christopher just wished he knew what they were thinking because the only thing worse than being out here was having no clue why.

Just before sunset, they stopped to set up camp beneath a stand of saplings. Of course, on Demeter 'sapling' meant the boles were a mere eighteen inches in diameter and the lowest branches fifteen feet over head. Christopher stood just beneath the trees at twilight numbly wondering how he could barely feel his feet, yet at the same time have them burn like fire.

Around him the soldiers raised a light-framed canopy, large enough for all of them to crowd beneath. He watched as they lowered the sides. The fabric was familiar. It woke the echo of a memory in his fogged brain. He reached out to rub a fold between his fingers. Again, familiar, and now he knew why. A plasticized version of the nylon fiber that had been used to form the body of a long-flying surveillance drone he'd served as project lead on. It had been just the edge they'd needed to successfully conclude the assignment. Not only was the material ultralight, but micro-circuitry woven among the threads was programmable for several key functions, from camouflaging to shielding to alternate energy absorption. When paired with the focused inboard lasers as an ignition source, latent energy could be converted into accessible power that could then be absorbed by the drone's thermal converter. Their goal had been to create a self-sustaining, self-repairing drone that could remain airborne for a year or more at a consistent altitude.

His team had succeeded.

He was very proud of that project; regretted having had to pass it on to Captain Linda Pierce, and the military's practical testing group. Professional rivalry aside, he more than liked Linda, though nothing much had come of it so far. Kind of hard when the military kept sending her off to remote locations to test his prototypes. Still, he always managed something to ensure she didn't forget about him. This time it had been a gaudy, glittery pin that proudly proclaimed *"I'm #2!"* He'd slipped it in with the transfer papers.

He couldn't wait to see what prank she pulled to get even. Who knew when that would be, though. Practical testing could take months. He hoped she was treating his baby with care. Just before the hand-off, a fire at the research facility had destroyed his final notes for the project before he was able to back them up.

He would have to reverse engineer the final stages from the prototype before the drones could go into production.

A familiar grip settled on Christopher's shoulder, yanking him around and away from his thoughts. "Perhaps I wasn't as clear as I believed I was, Mr. James, when this all started. When we had our talk about how to stay alive."

Exhausted and frustrated and more than a little annoyed, Christopher had less control of his tongue than usual. As in none. "Quite clear, Lieutenant Kolby, just not nearly complete enough."

Even as the words left his mouth, Christopher flinched. Kolby's jaw couldn't have jutted harder if it had been carved from granite. Still gripping Christopher's shoulder, he hauled him across to the edge of the canopy, as far as they could get from the other men.

"Excuse me?" Kolby's tone was low and even and completely at odds with his body language.

Sighing, Christopher dropped his gaze, before forcing it up again. It was in his nature to avoid conflict, but this wasn't the lab, and this wasn't going away. If he was already going to catch heat, he might as well speak his piece.

"Lieutenant, I'm not a soldier. I haven't had a soldier's training. I don't know how to move like you need me to. I don't have combat instincts. I haven't been trained to navigate terrain. I don't *know* what I need to watch for, or what I need to avoid."

He could tell by Kolby's furrowing brow that what he was trying to say wasn't getting through.

"Lieutenant Kolby, I'm a civilian, as much as we all need me to act like a soldier I'm never going to be good enough, especially compared to your men. I just don't have the skills." He raised his hands in the classic gesture of 'this is what you get'. "I'm an engineer. I'm assuming that's why I'm on this mission, why else would you go to the trouble... the *risk*... to haul me out here? But I don't have the data I need. I don't know what problem to bend my mind to. I need time to pull a solution out of my ass. If I'm going to be of any use to you, I have to know what's going on before it's in my face."

For a moment, Christopher thought he might have connected, then Kolby's military protocol clearly kicked in.

"Civilian or not, Mr. James, when you are in that uniform, on this mission... you are under my command!" Kolby barked out low and hard, his face bright red and his features twisted in anger. "I will tell you what you need to know, when you are authorized to know it. Until then, you bend that pointed little head of yours toward following orders before what's in your *face* is a shit storm!"

Acid bubbled in Christopher's gut as the lieutenant stalked away as far as the tent allowed. He stood there, pale and trembling in the wake of the conflict, forcing himself to remain standing straight. A taut silence hung in the air as the other soldiers went about their duties, clearly aware of the confrontation, but in no way reacting.

Without a word, Christopher moved to his belongings and spread out his bedroll. Before he could lay down, Kolby tossed a ration pack at him. It hit Christopher's chest hard enough it stung. His arms reflexively closed around it.

"Eat, *now*. We're not carrying your ass tomorrow."

Christopher's jaw clenched and his gut spasmed, but he followed orders.

They woke and broke camp before the sunrise did more than flirt with the horizon. Kolby ignored him—thank God—but the soldier from the day before, a dark-skinned man with RANDALL on his name tape and sergeant's stripes on his sleeve, pulled Christopher off to the side before they started the day's march.

"Think of it like a circuit board," Randall said, his gaze darting toward the lieutenant, like he was watching for one of his signals.

Christopher frowned. "What?"

"Moving through the terrain... it's tricky, you have to be careful to avoid notice... like when you're working on a circuit board. You need to know right where to move, and when to move, or you break or fry the circuits. Same with what we're doing here. Be alert, look for what's in your way... twigs beneath your feet, thorns on the bushes, those're the things that'll make you break your connection... so don't. Slow and steady does it, be alert, be focused, move carefully... like you're working on a circuit board."

He grinned, and Christopher had to grin back, not exactly feeling good about what lay ahead, but feeling better because Randall's advice made sense and even if it hadn't, the soldier... the *man*... was trying to help him out, like he had yesterday, when Christopher couldn't move.

"Now, pay attention," Randall went on. He moved his hands in a series of gestures, explaining what they stood for as he made each one. "Those are the ones Butter Bar is most likely to use." —it took Christopher a moment to realize Randall was referring to Kolby— "Anything else, you just drop down and stay still if you don't know what the signal means. That'll be safest."

Suddenly, Randall's expression changed, like he was listening to someone Christopher couldn't hear, and there was a faint twitch along his jaw. "Yessir," he muttered, then turned back to Christopher. "Don't worry, man, I'll be watchin' your back."

"Thank you," Christopher said with a nod. As the soldier started to move off, Christopher called to him, keeping his voice low. "Randall... please... what are we doing out here?"

For a moment it looked like the soldier would remain silent, but he darted a defiant look toward his lieutenant's back and then met Christopher's eye. When he spoke, his lips barely moved, "Command has lost contact with the practical testing group working on your UAV; they think the team's gone rogue and are using the drone to secure their position. We need you to crack the controls so we can take it back."

Christopher's chest tightened and his gut dropped as he thought of Linda. He couldn't say a word, couldn't catch a breath. He struggled a moment, then got himself under control. "You can't be serious!"

Across the headset came a burst of static, then Kolby's voice hissed, "Move your asses, NOW!"

Randall gave Christopher an understanding look and clapped his shoulder, then turned to fall into position. Christopher followed, taking his place behind Kolby without a word, his mind struggling with what he'd just been told.

As they made their way across the landscape, moving in at least an approximation of the soldiers' motions became easier as

Christopher kept Randall's metaphor in mind. He didn't relax—it was impossible to, between worrying about Linda, and wondering what the hell the true reason for the loss in communications was—but he fell into a rhythm that allowed him to take note of more of his surroundings. There seemed to be many instances of fire in the surrounding undergrowth, but none that had spread beyond the immediate source. He would have expected one spark would have set off a chain of wildfires, but there was no sign of it. Almost as if something squelched the fires before they could flare.

When they stopped for a brief break he edged closer to Randall. "Do you see that?" Christopher murmured, pointing to the remains of a tree. "It doesn't make sense. This whole area should be nothing but ash."

Before Randall could respond, Kolby shot them a hard look and gave the signal to head out.

Not long after, Samson's red light lit up.

Kolby's hand rose in a signal and all the soldiers took cover, their weapons raised as their eyes tracked the sky. Christopher scrambled after the lieutenant, crouching out of the way in the cover of a scorched bush nearby. He looked up, but all he saw were clouds drifting with the wind. On the other side of Kolby, Samson worked with focused intensity, adjusting and readjusting the settings on his machine until the green light reengaged.

Some of the tension in the group eased and Kolby gave the signal to proceed.

When Christopher tried to climb from hiding, the brambles caught in his clothes and some his flesh. Wincing as he struggled with the thorns, he forgot to watch his feet, to move careful. He cried out as he fell, his foot slipping on something smooth and rounded. The air rushed out of him as he hit the ground hard. Any breath he had left caught in his chest as he pushed himself up.

Blackened bone rested beneath his hand, but that was not what shook him to his core. Glittering between two ribs was a deformed novelty pin. He could almost make out the heat-distorted words *"I'm #2!"*. Or maybe that was his mind filling in the gaps he knew were there.

He was too shocked to cry out, but tears stung his lips on their way down his face. His throat rippled as his stomach heaved. He turned his head hard to the side so the vomit spattered the bushes and not the human remains strewn beneath him. With effort he got himself under control. Swiping his mouth across his uniform sleeve, Christopher reached down a trembling hand to clear away the ash from the fried radio frequency tags draped beside the blackened skull.

He read the first etched line: PIERCE, LINDA, and he could read no more. He knew why Command had lost communication with the practical testing group, and it wasn't because *they* had gone rogue. All the signs pointed to it, only Christopher hadn't known to make those connections before this grim discovery. The self-energizing drone he had helped create was responsible for the isolated fires in the area. It was also a killer. A cold, unfeeling killer, unable to distinguish between humans and an acceptable energy-conversion source. Because they hadn't thought to tell it how. Because *he* hadn't thought to tell it how.

Christopher's earlier pride turned to ashes in his mouth.

He looked up and met Kolby's furious gaze. Christopher didn't give a damn.

"We're here because the military lost communication with the testing facility."

The lieutenant didn't respond.

"They lost communications because everyone's *dead*."

Nothing.

"We have to destroy it," Christopher said.

Kolby glared down at him. "Destroy it? We're here to *retrieve* that valuable piece of military hardware. Now get up and get moving, or we leave you here."

At Kolby's words, Christopher went dead cold as he realized what the military intended.

More than lingering vomit left his mouth sour.

Not knowing what else to do, Christopher reached out and took Linda's pin and her tags, and stowing them in his bag. Only then did he scramble to his feet and fall back in line, hands clutching the straps of the rucksack containing his tablet computer. His mind was a jumble, leaping from one detail to the next, making unexpected connections as only an engineer's could.

A plan took loose form as they made their way closer to the military's practical testing facility.

Maybe facility was the wrong word; the place was a fortress. Shielded walls, (formerly) electrified gate, security doors half a foot thick. To all appearances, the place was better defended than the proverbial Fort Knox. Or it had been.

Christopher had no clue how many personnel had been stationed here, but the piles of scorched bone dotting the courtyard brought bile to his throat, even without counting them. When they made it to the entrance, the soldiers took up a defensive circle around Kolby as he entered a code into the security pad. As he waited, Christopher noted scorch marks along the walls, mostly concentrated around the light stanchions. They were shielded, but the hardest hit had failed, leaving shattered glass on the courtyard below, glittering like smoky diamonds among the ash. In places, the shielding had melted away, leaving fused circuits and slagged wiring exposed.

Christopher's mind recalled Randall's stealth metaphor and made another unanticipated leap, his plan gaining cohesion.

The security door opened and they scrambled inside. Or most of them did. Behind them a beam of laser light shot down from above, catching Samson. The tracker-slash-monitor he'd carried across the wilds smashed down on the marble courtyard as the soldier ignited too quickly to even scream. Christopher stared on in horror as a piece of the sky came down and sucked the energy out of the flame until it guttered out, leaving a fresh pile of scorched bones among the others.

"Secure that door! Move it!" Kolby ordered the remaining men.

Christopher just turned and stared at the lieutenant, shaking his head at Kolby's lack of regard.

Kolby stared back in a challenge that Christopher didn't understand.

"Time to do your job, James," Kolby ordered, breaking the heavy silence. "Get up into that control room and bring that bird down nice and easy so we can get it back to Command."

Only an extreme effort of will kept Christopher's jaw from dropping in outrage. Kolby had in no way acknowledged Samson's loss. When had men become throw-away commodities? Without a word, Christopher turned away and headed in the direction Kolby had pointed, stopping only to pick up the rucksack he hadn't realized he'd dropped. Randall stood beside it.

Christopher met his eye and saw a kindred resolve in the soldier's gaze. That could have been any of their bones gracing the courtyard.

"Don't worry," Randall said as he reached down and shouldered the bag, "I got your back."

They exchanged the subtlest of nods before they both climbed the stairs to the control room, but Christopher said nothing until the door closed behind them, blocking out the sound of Kolby shouting orders below.

In the sudden silence, Christopher scrambled to connect his tablet computer to the local network, knowing he likely only had a short time before Kolby or one of the others came bursting in to... *supervise.*

"Randall," Christopher called out as he waited for his system to boot up. "I need you to guard the door, buy me some more time."

"What are you doing?"

"Making sure my life's work doesn't become my life's shame," Christopher answered. "That drone needs to be taken out. It's like a vicious dog, turned on its owner. You put the dog down the first time, you don't wait to see if it does it again."

Randall went silent a moment, as if deciding what he should or shouldn't say. "They tried that already, the testing group, before Command ordered them to desist."

"Fuck Command!"

Randall look startled at Christopher's uncharacteristic outburst. Christopher hung his head, shaking it slowly from side to side. "That's my dog. I made it. I'm responsible for..." his throat closed on the words that would haunt him until his dying day. "...every person that beast killed to keep itself in the air. Every one of them... what is it you call it? Friendly fire. I can't make up for that, but I sure as hell can put that dog down. I built the thing! I know it inside and out, I sure as hell know where the kill switch is... I just need the time to flip it."

Randall nodded sharply, then headed for the door. Trusting him, Christopher turned back to his computer, fingers skittering over the keys so fast even he could barely distinguish the individual clicks. Kill switch had been too generous a term, the military would have never authorized such a thing, but most engineers in research and development planned contingencies, just in case everything unexpectedly went to hell.

Christopher heard shouting out in the corridor but tuned it out as he overrode the drone's autonomous systems to take control of the inboard lasers, retracting them into their protective default position. He then shut down the safety protocols to activate those lasers, frying the delicate inner workings and igniting the nylon skin. For the briefest of moments Christopher's "dog" fed off itself before the system red-lined and the drone crashed to the cobbles below, sending a noxious black cloud up into the sky.

As the door to the control room burst open, Christopher hung his head, a single tear falling on the keys as he hit his personal kill switch, wiping his computer hard drive.

"What did you do?"

Straightening, Christopher turned and gave Kolby a hard look.

"I corrected the mistake I never should have made."

Christopher James walked right past Lieutenant Kolby and left the fortress, heading the opposite direction from where they'd left the transport, the memory of Linda Pierce's remains haunting his every step.

Travellin' Show

A Tale of the Kalderas Clan

GYPSIES, TRAMPS AND THIEVES... IT WAS THE TITLE OF AN ANCIENT song from the twentieth century that echoed with my voice, my life—for all that the singer was a woman, and planet-bound. She and I shared the same nose, and perhaps a dark, unfathomable gaze, but not much else, other than the scul of that song. I don't even know her name, though we had fragments of old dig-vids of her singing the words in deep, whisky-rich tones.

I hated her for seeing so clearly. For making me see so clearly.

For many Ages of Man, the human race had longed for the stars. I had them and didn't much care for it. Me, I wanted dirt beneath my feet miles deep, moving in a slow, massive spin I couldn't hope to feel were I as still as dead. I wanted to look up and see the stars twinkle and find nothing but satisfaction in the fact that I could see them through the filter of a planet's sky. I wanted roots, just once in my life, if only for a moment.

I believed someday I would. Someday... if I had to live up to every rotten thing they said about us. The kindest folk said we were all glitz, glam, and sham; everyone else... well, you get the idea.

You see, the frontier of space was much more dangerous than any similar state of existence planetside. People were desperate, harsh, and took what they could get in the way of easing the darkness all around them. They got to believing everyone else would gladly do them worse, so do it first.

That's why there are rules that every Caravan holds to and ruthlessly enforces. Cheat us, and we're gone; harm us, and we're gone for good; kill one of our own, and don't ever sleep again.

The dark is deep and cold. We—the Rom—are a touch of golden warmth in the black, a laugh when the universe is crying, passion where most bodies are worn down to indifference. We are welcome everywhere... once night falls and the stage lights are lit, the carnie booths are pitched, and everyone young and decent is tucked away in bunks. We bring the things that can't be had, the little pleasures, moments of forgetfulness, news from home ironically delivered by those who have never had one, unless you count the caravan ships.

No matter how they looked down on us, there wasn't a man jack in space who would risk being stricken from our travel circuit by mistreating us.

Or so we believed.

"Paolo, come on... it's time to dock." Terlinda startled me as her voice crackled from the wall comm. My sister sounded annoyed.

I said nothing and finished shaving, rebelliously scraping an antique straight razor across my scalp with slow care, revealing smooth, bare skin that was every inch a lie. On the Kalderaš Caravan there wasn't a patch of skin on any of us above the age of three that wasn't tattooed with vibrant, nanite-embedded ink. Some claimed it was because in space we couldn't paint our caravans as our ancestors did, so we patterned our skin instead.

Maybe that was true, but more importantly the tattoos were both warning and defense, though none but our own were aware of the latter. As far as the universe was concerned it was just one more difference between us and them. An easy way to tell who not to trust... or piss off, but other than that, just elaborate skin art.

Little did they know.

The markings of the Rom did more than earn us those labels of glitz, glam, and sham... at a silent mental command the nanites in the ink projected sensory holograms, creating the il-lusion of hair, clothes, and even ready-changing features by means of hard-light holo-projections intricate enough to fool even complex electronic recording devices. Mostly we used it to enhance our performances, but it came in equally handy when we had a need to vanish without a trace, or appear as something other than what we are.

The universe knew us by our ink. This is why—when not among the *gadje*... outsiders—my silent protest was to appear unmarked by any color that wasn't flesh, and to retain the growth of hair most of my people had chemically switched off as a practicality of traveling in space. Yes, it meant I had to shave before docking with other vessels or outposts for a show, but I still held the hope that my life would be different someday, and even just that fringe of hair that was not illusion made me feel it might be attainable.

Little did *I* know.

"Paolo! Now!" This time Terlinda snapped at me from the cabin hatch, sending my hand and the razor it held sluicing sideways in a shallow cut across my scalp.

"Ah!" I hissed with the pain, however brief; I felt a sharp tingle across my damaged skin as diligent nanites rushed to repair their roof. Glaring back at her, I took the time to clean the blade and carefully put it away before rinsing the blood and shaving foam from my head. In moments, the only clue I'd bled myself was the fading metallic tang on the air.

"What is the point of all of this?" she asked, her hand gesturing at my illusion of normalcy, annoyance and exasperation coloring her words. "It isn't like you will ever fit among them, no matter what you look like. All you do is waste our time. And cost us double docking fees for holding up station traffic."

I didn't bother to argue anymore. It was an old battle of strike and counterstrike etched into the temporal memory of the ship a thousand-fold. In silence, I moved past her, lowering my head to kiss her brow—which annoyed her further, as I'd had a growth spurt that left me six inches to the advantage of her own five-feet. While she sputtered, I strode down the corridor toward the docking portal and my assigned task. We were not at risk of fines, despite Terlinda's claims; not this time and never again since the first time, before I'd learned to feel the changes in the drive that indicated power-down in preparation for docking.

Since becoming attuned to those subtle variations in the engines' sounds I have never, ever been late to my post.

Terlinda growled behind me, her breath huffing ever so slightly as she hurried to catch up. "Are you so ashamed of what we are that you want to be like them? Are you so eager to be *gadje*?" She spat the word, a bitter insult when applied to one of our own.

What she said stopped me, but it was what I heard beneath the words that had me turn back to her. Her surface scorn mingled with a deeper hurt that she tried to hide, bringing glimpses to the surface. I met her eyes, so like my own, deep and dark, if rather more deceptively doe-like. I closed my own against the pain she let me see there. It nearly gutted me to be the cause of it. She was like my own mother, for ours had long ago joined the stars as we never could this side of life. How to explain to her and not hurt her more?

"*Camlo*,"—*lovely one*—"there is nothing about shame in this... of any of you or myself." I struggled for the words to explain what I had yet to make clear to anyone in my clan. "Have you never dreamed to stand upon a planet? To feel its unmoving mass beneath your feet? To see the grass and birds and a proper sunrise? To breathe the crisp, clean flavor of natural air and not feel the constant threat of vacuum weighing down on you?"

For just a moment in my life I wanted to know what it felt like not to wander. Had my sister never felt the same?

Before she could answer me, the rumble of the engines shifted to a subtle drone warning me I'd no more time. I left Terlinda with confusion in her eyes as I spun around and hurried to my post before I proved her right about the fines.

The Midway Outpost was exactly that: midway between Earth and the furthest colony. It orbits a planet called Xerxes where there are a few scientific installations and one military complex, but not much else, according to the spatial-net. I have never been there before—the planet or the outpost. It takes a long time to tramp around the universe. The last time the Kalderaš Caravan had docked here was sixteen years ago; I had not even been born.

With a swiftness gained by much repetition, we unloaded our wares and trappings from the ship and shuttled everything we would need to set up our traveling show to an emptied assembly bay at the center of the outpost.

Whether founded or unfounded, the reputation of our kind preceeded us. We were watched over closely as we went about our business. Some of us too closely. Each time Terlinda left the Caravan the eyes of the male outpost personnel followed her. I did not like the looks on their faces. Though I was only fifteen and my sister nearing twenty, I knew as her brother it was my place to protect her. What was more, I loved her as I loved none other, and God help anyone who offered her insult or harm.

When she next came down the ramp I walked beside her wearing the appearance of a man taller and more muscled than I could ever hope to be. The tattoos on the seeming—different from those on my actual body—were bold and agressive, all stark black lines and bright blues and reds, like the warnings given off by the skin of a poisonous toad. I didn't need any help from the nanites to darken my expression as I made sure to catch the eye of each of those men staring. Some of them looked amused and went back to what they were doing, others sneered and kept on looking, some rare few were clearly embarrassed and nodded respectfully in our direction before turning away; none of them challenged my silent warning.

And still, for the balance of the offload I kept that image of power and strength. The effort wore on me as I had to remember my perceived physical boundaries, as opposed to the actual ones.

"You are an ass," Terlinda murmured under her breath at me.

"Love you too," I grumbled back while maintaining my looming presence and ducking under a hatchway that I would have otherwise walked beneath with no problem. The others of the clan politely took no notice of my ruse, though for one who knew how to tell they were clearly amused.

Finally, with the pack-out complete, we set about transforming the lackluster bay into a cross between a gypsy carnival and a homeworld bazaar. Lights and bobbles and fabrics in bright, vibrant colors were swiftly deployed and arranged. Right at the entry hatch the other boys and I set up the three-sided square of stalls. The moment we finished one the older women filled it up with luxury goods while we moved onto the next. The stalls were simple frames of aluminum 'bamboo' draped with colorful silk.

In addition to ambiance, they served to block the view and path of those who had not paid to enter the carnival. Beyond this screen Father and my uncles were raising two larger, more private tents, off to either side of the bay—one for business such as the sending and receiving of personal messages, discreetly purchasing certain goods, or treating ills the crew could not or would not bring to the Medbay; the other was for entertainments for which the crew must pay an extra fee to view, such as the fancy dancing and the curiosity acts. Beyond all of that, the rest of the space was for feasting and public dancing. The younger women were in charge there and had already created of the bare, serviceable bay an exotic gathering area that bore little resemblance to its earlier state.

Wiping sweat from my holographic chin—in truth, my damp brow—I watched as my sister and cousins set up the fireboxes, our version of the traditional firepits that would have been found at a true carnival. Already the scent of spices and meat were on the air and they hadn't even started cooking. My mouth watered. At a table beside Terlinda, other women of the clan set out specialty foods that would soon go on to the encased grill as regulations forbid open flames in the oxygen-rich, canned atmosphere of the outpost.

Terlinda laughed as she stoked the coals and started loading prepared kabobs in the transition area to be moved on to the grill. She made a face at me when she caught me staring. I didn't mind because her eyes were filled with love; it was good to see her without the scowl I usually managed to put on her face. Turning away I bent to clean up the last of the tools we had used to set up the bazaar. As I did, I noticed one of the watchers from earlier nearby. His gaze hooded... one corner of his mouth barely upturned. I did not care for what I saw. The man watched the women preparing the food.

"Can I help you?" I asked, stepping between him and them.

He smirked. "Naw, just working up an appetite."

My jaw tightened at the many ways that could be taken. "If you don't mind, we aren't quite ready for business yet. Thank you."

"So, tell me," the man said, his expression growing sly and a touch hungrier. "Which tent do we go to for a little time with one of the girls?"

It took effort to keep my tone neutral. I may not have succeeded. "None of them. Romany women don't sell their virtue."

The crewman looked confused, and then angry. I was fortunate that I still wore my more intimidating, if illusionary, seeming from earlier or perhaps things would have gone differently. As it was, he lifted his chin and just barely his lip in the ghost of a sneer, his arms crossing over his chest. In response, I sent a subtle command to the nanites beneath my skin to flex my holographic muscles. I held the man's gaze. I saw evil in the soul staring back at me.

Things could have gotten ugly if the station's head of security had not come through the hatch as we stared one another down. The watcher's gaze flickered to the newcomer; mine stayed steady on the man.

"Everything okay, Crewman Tran?"

"Yes, sir," Tran answered as his arms dropped to his side and he turned to salute his superior. It was then that I noticed the security patch on his uniform and cursed beneath my breath. "Just about to inspect this gypsy's load, make sure nothing that belongs to the station *accidentally* got mixed up with it."

I must have growled at the offense because both the crewman and his boss looked at me intently.

"Paolo," Father's voice cracked sharply from behind me. "Let security look, then get those tools back to the Caravan and put away."

With a subtle understanding, the head of security gave a little wave of his hand, a polite smile on his face. "No, that won't be necessary. I'm sure you all have plenty to do to ready things for tonight. We won't hold you."

Startled, I looked up and met his eye. His smile deepened into one with more warmth. I suddenly got the impression I didn't fool him. He nodded toward the hatch and stepped to the side. As I walked away, slightly trembling in reaction, I spared a glance for my sister; she looked safe and happy, surrounded by our family as they finished the final preparations for the carnival. With that sight firm in my mind, I was content to turn and go.

As I moved down the corridor I heard the officer speaking behind me: "Tran, your new orders have come in. You're being rotated planetside; report to the XO for your papers and a shuttle requisition."

I resisted the urge to turn and smirk back at that asshole, who would now miss out on all the carnival did have to offer.

It was petty, but my only satisfaction.

By the time I stowed the tools and endured the latest lecture from my father, who had followed me back to the Caravan, it was time to change. The carnival had been running several hours and shortly the special performances would begin. I once more appeared as myself, brightly colored and intricately marked, swirls and ancient markings clear upon my skin, with a star-burst at the center of my forehead that subtly sparkled as the nanites beneath the skin released tiny charges of light like controlled static, only without the shocking sensation. My garb, while suitably flamboyant in cut, was subtle in color. I wore a long open vest of raw amber silk belted over a crisp, white shirt with billowing sleeves and a front that opened in a deep vee to my navel. My pants were supple black leather that just barely gleamed in the subdued light of the Caravan. They were close-fitting, but soft as kid, and no impediment to movement; no small consideration, as I was a tumbler tonight. Finished with my preparations, I went to join the rest of the special performers, who were gathering at the exit ramp.

It disturbed me not to see my sister. She loved the life we led, the performing, the glamour, the thrill. In all my given memory, I couldn't recall a time when she hadn't been the first to the ramp, in her jewel-tone scarves and bangles, flowing skirts and soft, curl-toed slippers. My eyes scanned the group again. All there, but for Terlinda.

"Father..." I called. There must have been some warning in my voice.

He turned from where he talked with Uncle Tomias, the two of them reviewing the entertainment planned for the night, as they always did. Father's brow gathered in concern, the pattern there wrinkled with the expression. "Paolo?"

"I don't see Terlinda."

I could not read his expression, which disturbed me, but his tone remained calm as he said, "Go check her cabin, please." I hurried to do as he bid.

She was not there. But her costume was, waiting on a peg beside her door, ready for the night's performance. I snatched one bangled scarf and hurried back to where my family waited. I did not even have to speak.

As if I even could.

My father ordered me to stay behind. He knew. He knew better than I did what would happen if he let me free. If we discovered the worst.

I tried to obey. I told myself that I should be there when she returned, as surely she would. My Terlinda should not come back to an empty ship with whatever grief she may have suffered.

No. I should not think such thoughts. And yet my heart knew no innocent thing had kept Terlinda from all she loved in life. Guilt burned like a brand inside me. I paced and tore at my clothes, battered my mind for any clue hiding there. My thoughts kept coming back to Tran and the look in his eye. The sickness in his soul.

There was no staying put.

Throwing off my costume I pulled on an outfit of all black cotton, close and tight as a second skin, nothing to impede me, whatever I must do. From a locker beneath my bunk I drew a matching set of antique throwing knives I'd inherited from my grandfather, and he from his. They were the only things I had that resembled weapons. I'd been well-taught in their use.

I normally only used them when I performed one of the curiosity acts.

Without a second thought I belted them around my waist. An order to the nanites both hid them from view and cloaked my features in a nondescript face made up of pieces melded from the crew, creating an appearance vaguely familiar but known to none. Armed and armored against resistance I circumvented the lock on the hatch and went out into the station, seeking out the only one who might help me.

Even armed with the directions to his personal cabin, it took some time to find the head of security. More than it had taken to find his name—Stan Wilkes—which I carefully pilfered along with the rest of my information from the station system using hacking skills learned at my granddad's side.

Wilkes did not seem surprised to see me.

"I expected you sooner, Paolo," he said, as I slid through the hatch to his cabin.

I went still, the holo image fluxing around me in my confusion. Then the man blinked and I could clearly see the flutter of lenses flick across his eye. I dropped the seeming.

"I wouldn't be a very good head of security if I didn't have the latest tech, would I?"

He started to rise. I locked my jaw and braced myself for attack, but he sat back down, placing his hands in full view palm down upon his desk. "It's okay. I'm not against you. Your father has been to see me," he explained. "My men are searching now, your people with them; I'm only here to review the security feed, or I would be searching right along with..."

I cut him off. "It was Tran."

Wilkes sighed and lowered his head in acknowledgement. When he looked up I wanted to snarl at what I saw. "It was him!" I stalked forward, my fists clenched and my expression as twisted as my gut. My sister was in the hands of a beast, I had no doubt, and as clear as I knew that, I knew just from looking at him that the man before me was going to say there was nothing he could do.

I blinked and stopped dead. Without seeming to move at all, Wilkes had drawn a riot gun on me. I cursed and stood there trembling, waiting for the door behind me to open and security forces to hurry in. Instead, Wilkes placed the non-lethal weapon on the desk and slowly rose to his feet.

"I suspect you are right, but I can't prove it, and Tran left the outpost less than twenty standard minutes after I sent you back to your ship. The feed *seems* to support that he left alone."

My knees buckled at his words. I would have fallen without the edge of the desk.

That had been over four hours ago. That was when I understood Wilkes's expression: his men weren't on a search and rescue. They were on a search and *recover*.

Something inside me wanted to howl. To scream and cry and curl into a ball. That something was frozen in ice, locked deep down at the angry core of me. I locked gazes with Wilkes and waited for him to say what I knew was to come.

His voice sounded just above a whisper. "I can't go after him based on the feed, even though I suspect it's been altered... any more than I could go after you for stealing a shuttle, *if the feed said it wasn't you.*"

I straightened, then nodded, before turning and walking out the door.

By the time I hit the corridor, I wore another face.

Hijacking a shuttle was easier than it should have been. But I guess I shouldn't have been surprised; after all, the head of security was unofficially supportive of my efforts. Still, it felt like a cheat. Not that I dwelled on that then, not with my sister's well-being dependent on my success. Or so I told myself.

There wasn't anyone among the Rom above the age of eight that didn't know how to pilot a shuttle. Personally, I could fly anything, upto and including the Caravan itself. A shuttle was nothing. Now, figuring out Tran's flight path... that took a little more finesse. Not the one he'd logged with flight control, but the one the tracer in his craft automatically recorded. Most people didn't even know those existed.

I'm not most people.

Even so, an ordinary hack wouldn't have gotten me the data. That was why I'd lifted Wilkes's security code earlier, when I figured out where to find him. I suspect even then I'd had his unofficial support.

I'd just left the stratosphere when the tracker on my shuttle pinged the one Tran had taken to the surface. It appeared by the mapping display that he had set down in a secluded clearing about ten miles from the complex he had been assigned to. I tried not to think of why.

It never occurred to me I was, in part, about to achieve my dream. I was too focused to really notice. Or wonder. Too tormented to care.

The more I descended the harder it was to breathe. The more my heart pounded. The harder it was to think. I dropped my engines as low as I could without stalling and glided the craft in, landing about a quarter mile from Tran's location, out of sight of the shuttle.

The hatch on my vessel cycled open and I barely felt I had the strength to climb to my feet. The pull of full gravity was like granite ballast filling me up. The air burned my lungs as I screamed in rage. I had not considered the effects of planetfall on a body that had never before left space.

I forced myself to my feet and somehow made it to the open hatch. If my body were not well-honed by the rigors of performance I could not have managed even that.

I did not so much climb to the surface as tumble down the stairs. The natural light nearly blinded me. When I manage to gain my feet, slow step by slow step, I dragged myself in the direction of the other shuttle. The hatch was open when I got there. I just stood and stared, scarcely believing how both simple and hard this journey had been. In truth, I dreaded what I would find. Dreaded more what I might not. What if she wasn't here? What if I had made the wrong choice and Terlinda suffered for it?

I gritted my teeth and climbed the steps to the shuttle hatch. I was no more than halfway when a sound came to my ears. Snoring. Faint snoring, broken up by a snuffle and occasionally a murmur.

Yes, it took me that long to climb.

When finally I reached the top I slumped against the hatch, not caring if my quarry should see me. It took forever for my eyes to adjust again to darkness.

Inside, deep at the angry core of me, I died.

On the floor of the shuttle lay Tran fast asleep and naked.

Beside him... my Terlinda, her eyes vacant and filmed, the damage to her bare body half-knitted by the nanites before they too began to die. The colors of the ink beneath her skin were fading without the bots' inner brilliance. Tears streamed down my face, but I did not feel them. My chest heaved and my eyes glazed; I did not even realize as my right hand fell to the hilt of one of my throwing knives.

Tran twitched, and snorted, and some benumbed portion of my brain railed at the wrongness of that. Muscles and reflexes trained by countless performances and an even greater number of practices fought against the weight of gravity to do as they had been taught.

The Caravans hold to a code: Cheat us, and we're gone; harm us, and we're gone for good; kill one of our own, and don't ever sleep again.

We would never return to Midway Outpost.

I would never again set foot on dirt.

We left in the night. It was simple, even on a fortified outpost, as long as you had the skill to bypass the systems keeping you in dock. I did, but I wasn't in any shape to. Hell, I didn't even know how I'd gotten us back. That didn't quite matter, though, as we seemed to have retained a certain unofficial support.

Someone else stepped up and unlocked the gate.

In the finest tradition of gypsies throughout history, we faded away among the stars like a memory to protect one of our own.

That would be me. Paolo.

I killed a man, a *gadje*, a vicious dog who behaved worse by far than anything people said of the Rom. I don't even know his first name. Frankly, I don't care. What I know is that he brutalized my sister and she died at his hand.

Tran should have remembered not to sleep.

CASUALTIES OF WAR

An Alliance Archives Adventure

The first casualty of war is innocence.
—Platoon

THE SOUNDS OF FIGHTING WERE LONG SILENCED, REPLACED BY THE squabbling of scavengers; birds and beasts that Devon assumed were little different from those found picking over any other battlefield throughout time, regardless of the planet. No people had come yet to claim, strip, or add to the corpses, but he gripped the stock of his useless weapon tight, just in case, as he peered into the dark watching for any motion.

A glance at the stars showed a faint glow to his left, on the horizon. Not long until dawn, when he could get a few hours of rest before the daylight creatures came for their share of the leavings. He had to wonder if he would be counted a leaving by then and shuddered, gasping as his wounds shot sharp pains up his legs and into his groin in response to the motion.

He gritted his teeth and forced himself still. It took long moments and left him exhausted. When he managed it, he lay there and stared up at the sky wondering how the hell war had become any more pertinent in his life than the history his granddad had taught him.

Even now it did not feel real, despite his injuries, yet the memory of the Dominion convoy rolling into town haunted him awake or sleeping, until panic constantly churned his gut. Grim, dusty soldiers with their rifles in their grips instead of slung across their backs. Battered jeeps and large, open transports, some piled with supplies, others holding men and strong-backed youths like himself. Though he and his granddad were new to

Demeter, some of them Devon had recognized from trading with neighboring towns. Granddad had tried to sneak him to the edge of the forest where he could hide in the far-up canopy of the towering trees, but soldiers had been waiting on the other side of the settlement as well.

Devon's last memory of his granddad was his crumpled body on the ground, blood flowing over his face and into the dirt. Others from the town had rushed to help the old man up, but the transport they had dumped Devon into was already driving away.

A dry, cracking sob tore from his raw throat and he bit off any others inclined to follow before he drew the attention of the scavengers, he heard but could not see. His heart pounded as he listened for sounds of the beasts approaching. For now, they seemed more interested in the corpses. Or perhaps they just had not come across him yet, the scent of his dried blood no competition for that of the carrion strewn over the fields in front of him.

He leaned back against the boulder where he'd dragged himself for shelter; grateful for the protection at his back. As his heartbeat slowed, he noticed a faint, warm pulse against his chest, coming from the Alliance tags hanging around his neck. They weren't there to fool anyone. The Dominion officers gave out extra rations to the conscripts for every set of tags turned in. This was the first Devon had ever claimed. They would never know the kill wasn't his.

Not that Devon was likely to have a chance to collect the bounty.

He shuddered—gasped—and resumed watching the dark for motion until dawn broke and the scavengers returned to their dens or wherever they went to ground. His eyes burned from staring into nothing and the cold cramped his hand around the gun stock, but what was one more ache against a multitude of others.

Despite his best efforts, Devon succumbed to sleep.

"Scan again, dammit!" Major James Rowland knew he was being irrational, but he would not... *could* not leave without being certain. The soldier at the con targeted the sensors on the planet below. Keying in the coordinates of the last engagement, he transmitted the master code and ran a search for any active radiofrequency, or RF, tags, which only broadcast active biometrics when pinged by the proper signal from the orbiting transport. Rowland sat rigid, eyes on his console where the results would also display.

The screen before him remained dark.

He swore with enough heat that the command crew went still and silent.

"Expand the scan one klick on all perimeters."

His jaw clenched and he closed his eyes, praying for the one blip that would save him from having to break his sister Kelly's heart.

Devon woke to another shudder. He swallowed a moan and forced himself to be motionless, riding through the pain. The sun was nearly overhead. It lit the horrific scene before him in bright, unforgiving light. Scavengers were thick on the battlefield, fighting over the remains of soldiers he'd fought beside... and against. If any had survived the battle beyond himself, there was no sign that he could see. For now, the creatures still seemed unaware of his presence. Or they just weren't interested yet. Apparently, fear was none so tempting as the pungent stench of rotting flesh. The smell had begun to ripen until he nearly gagged on it, though he had dragged himself quite some distance from the field of engagement. He squeezed his eyes shut tight for just a moment and wished with all his heart that when he opened them, he'd see his own rough room and his granddad in the doorway nagging him to get up.

But no, he was too old for wishes, if too young for war.

A few hundred yards away a crab-like creature pulled the armor off the remains of an Allied soldier while smaller, bug-like scavengers darted in to snatch away the leavings. Devon turned his gaze away, but kept the creature in the corner of his eye lest it move toward him next. His grip tightened on the rifle still clutched in his hands.

He forced those thoughts away and glanced up at the sky. The weather was clear now, but he still ached to his bones with the chill of last night's rain. The rock at his back slowly baked in the sun. Devon could barely feel its warmth, as another shiver sent sharp shards of pain through his body.

With his free hand he reached into his shirt and gripped the tags hanging there. One was the standard identification tag worn by all soldiers, the other a non-military issue holochip. His finger found the trigger and he allowed himself a brief moment of humanity.

"I love you, come home to me," whispered a sweet, youthful voice, just barely loud enough to reach his ears.

The words hurt almost as much as his broken body.

He couldn't say why, given they weren't for him. Or maybe that was it. Tears stung his eyes and his lip trembled as he stared the truth in the eye. Unless his granddad had survived, no one waited for him to come home. And the young woman unknowingly giving him the comfort of another human voice? She was doomed to disappointment. The Dominion had screwed them both over.

Devon gently triggered the recording again, not bothering to peer at the tiny flickering image dancing above his chest. He closed his eyes and let himself imagine someone waited.

"There! Right there!" Rowland leaned in close over the crewman's shoulder, his eyes on the blip on the screen signaling an active RF tag. Personnel data for Sergeant Justin Krougliak began to scroll down the screen beside the marker. Faint tremors went through Rowland as the sudden relief flooded his body with endorphins.

He wouldn't be forced to tell his sister she was a widow.

"Bring up topography for that location and send it to my console."

As the crewman followed his orders, Rowland went back to his station.

Calling up the biometric data being broadcast by Justin's tag, Rowland reviewed the information: fever, irregular heart rate, reduced oxygen levels. Concerning, but not alarming. And yet he felt a sense of urgency that was not altogether objective. He keyed in an alert for any radical changes and toggled the biometric screen down, switching to the topographical data that had just finished loading.

"Okay, Richey, power up your bird and deliver that medi-mech," Rowland called over his shoulder to the drone pilot as he examined their target area. While the battle had taken place on a relatively flat field, the RF signal came from a rocky area some distance outside of the combat zone. They wouldn't be able to land the drone in that region without risking damage to the 'mech that could render it unable to complete its mission. He scanned the region for a suitable landing zone closest to the RF signal. "Here are your coordinates. You land that drone nice and neat and fast then instruct that 'mech to double-time it to target. We have a soldier to save."

"You got it, PM."

Rowland swallowed a growl. PM, short for puppet master. Usually, he was good-natured about the men calling him that. Today it just got under his skin, salting the wound, as it were. Just another reminder that the only medicine he got to practice anymore was by proxy, through the robotic interface of the medi-mechs that had replaced live combat medics. And even then, only if the 'mech couldn't handle the situation on its own.

Hell, the only way he got to connect with his patients at all was through the video interface built into the 'mech's chassis. Not for the first time Rowland chafed at his growing sense of detachment fed by this particular military directive. Practicing medicine by remote wasn't what he'd trained for. Command insisted there was no significant impact on treatment. Rowland couldn't say one way or the other on that score, but he knew for a fact there were certain things the waldos just could not do effectively, even under the guidance of actual medical personnel, and that could be the difference between saving a soldier and burying one. Rowland kept his objections to himself, though, rather than risk reassignment to some post where he would make even less of a difference.

He pulled up the drone's frequency on his screen and mapped its trajectory. Something was causing drift. It was going to miss the target, either slamming into the rocks or landing on the wrong side of them. Rowland's jaw tightened and his brow furrowed. "Lieutenant..." he started to snap at Richey, but left the rest of his reprimand unsaid as a course correction already registered on the screen before him. Pushing away from his station, he stood abruptly. "I'm going down to medbay. I'll monitor from there."

Rowland's mood did not improve as tension noticeably left the command crew at his departure.

Devon jerked back to full consciousness as the snarling and snapping of beasts drew nearer. Something resembling a pit bull crossed with a beetle faced off with one of the mega-crabs. Devon made the mistake of watching too closely. He gagged hard as he looked away. What he wouldn't give for the familiar creatures back on Earth. At least those made sense to him.

When would they reach him? When would he become the prize two beasts fought for? Despite the pain, he lay flat and wedged himself as far beneath the curved base of his sheltering boulder as he could, until he presented little target that was not protected. His right hand clutching the rifle jerked up until the stock angled like a shield across his vitals. With his other hand he reached into the ordnance pouch at his side, fumbling as his fingers trembled, but still managing to work the flap open. He felt inside and let out a shaky sigh of relief. Inside were three flash grenades, all the Dominion would allow barely trained conscripts such as himself. Probably afraid that anything more lethal would be more likely to take out their own platoon instead of the Allied forces. Still, what he had might be enough to buy him time. The noise and smoke one grenade generated should scare off anything that came too nearby. Not yet, though.

He blinked and struggled to focus. The sounds of squabbling had gotten louder, but the beasts kept their distance, for now. They were the least of his worries, though, as he realized sweat beaded his forehead, except where it ran a trail past the edge of his helmet and down his neck. Yet the rest of him continued to shiver and shudder. If he dared let go of his gear long enough to touch it, he was sure his wounded leg would burn his fingertips. As it was, a faint odor crept toward his nose, more noticeable in the close confines. At this point he'd be damned lucky to keep the leg, if he came out of this alive at all.

A low-level hum caught his ear as something passed overhead, barely heard. His gaze snapped to the sky and his head swam with the sudden motion. For a moment he thought he'd be sick, but he swallowed hard. His heart raced with the sudden need to get out of sight, only there was no more shelter than this slight overhang, and thanks to the damage to his leg he wasn't going anywhere else. It had been all he could manage just to gain what ground he had before the infection had set in.

Resigned, Devon readied his grenades, gripped his weapon, and hunkered down in his makeshift bivouac, not sure what would be worse: being found, or being forgotten.

If Rowland was the puppet master, then the medi-mech was his Pinocchio. Patterned off the historic packbots employed in the twentieth and twenty-first centuries to clear combat zones of explosive devices, the 'mechs were programmed with a rudimentary AI and a knowledge database comparable to the training a field medic would receive. Unleashed in a combat zone after battle, they could home in on RF tags broadcasting biometrics that matched programed profiles indicating combat trauma of some sort. Upon reaching its target they were capable of performing basic triage and handling most non-critical wounds. For everything else there was him... or others like him... medical personnel parked safe in orbit, sitting at a terminal capable of connecting to the medi-mech and taking over its functions to perform more complex field surgeries, as needed, but only in the most urgent circumstances where a soldier could not be medevac'd out of the combat zone before receiving treatment.

Rowland held his breath as the drone landed and the semi-autonomous medi-mech self-deployed, releasing the lockdowns that joined it to the drone. More data scrolled across his monitor, fed to him direct from the 'mech; Environmental conditions, course adjustments, preliminary evaluations of the patient based on the biometric data the unit began receiving from the RF tag.

Stuck on the orbiting transport, Rowland's every muscle bunched and clenched with tension. Waiting did not suit him. He was a doer. To sit here two hundred miles above the planet, unable to get in there and do what he was trained for... There was nothing he hated more.

Tapping a few keys on his terminal he activated the observation camera, but not the reverse video feed. His gut clenched as the 'mech moved over the devastated landscape in the direction of the RF signal. The unit had an image stabilizer, but it could only do so much given the broken terrain. However, as the 'mech began moving past the remains of the fallen, Rowland gagged and looked away as the images came through more clearly than he was comfortable with. He was no stranger to the harsh reality of the battlefield, but right now he could not stomach the gazes of the dead, somehow both empty and accusing, one face practically unblemished while the next was cruelly butchered, postmortem. A searing guilt heated Rowland through as he realized what he felt most as the corpses scrolled by was relief that none of them were Justin. And yet each fallen soldier took on the shade of his brother-in-law's face until Rowland disabled the visual feed and set an alert to bring the camera back online once the 'mech reached target.

As he sat there waiting, he faced the hard fact that even principles fell casualty to war.

Devon woke to a gentle tug on his rifle, then a more serious yank. His grip tightened and he struggled to open his eyes, but they seemed crusted closed... or maybe they were just too heavy. For a moment he forgot why he wanted to open them. He started to drift off again when the stock was nearly jerked out of his hands.

"No!" he shouted. "Mine... mine." A sharp clack sounded close, followed by a loud snap, like steel links being hewn by a bolt cutter. Suddenly, Devon found himself holding just the butt of his weapon... and minus a piece of his thumb. He screamed and his eyes tore open. He could barely focus on the hellish figure before him, but he saw enough to recognize that it was one of the massive, crab-like creatures scavenging the battlefield. The other half of Devon's weapon was clutched in the creature's claw. Without a thought, Devon's good hand dove into the ordnance pouch closing on one of his flash grenades. He pulled the pin and rolled the cylinder as close to the creature as he could manage.

The force of the explosion sent his helmet crashing into the boulder behind him, but Devon barely felt a thing, temporarily blind, deaf, and sliding full speed into oblivion.

A sudden alert blared through medbay. On Rowland's monitor, the window displaying Justin's biometric data auto-opened. A series of updates scrolled down the screen: Elevated heart- and respiratory rate. Increased levels of stress hormones, followed by chemical indications of fresh injury.

Justin was under attack.

Before he was even finished interpreting the data, the medi-mech assessed the change in biometrics and triggered its combat protocol, picking up speed and activating defensive armaments.

As Rowland reengaged the 'mech's cameras, a second window opened on his screen. The remote visuals came back online. He had the sense that the devastation was much less once they passed the edges of the battlefield, but it was difficult to be sure with it moving by in such a blur. The terrain flew past as the 'mech ramped full speed toward Justin's location.

The image on Rowland's screen shook with sudden violence and a notation on the lower right frame of the window indicated the 'mech had fired its flechette cannon. His mouth went dry and his muscles tensed as the camera stabilized and the image of a massive bolt-cutter crab the size of a warthog played across the screen. The back of the brightly colored exoskeleton was blackened, with fluids and flesh pulping through the holes and cracks left by the flechette rounds. Inexplicably, the bottom of the creature was also blackened and riddled with cracks. The creature's upraised claw still held the remains of a rifle.

Rowland's brow furrowed when he realized the weapon was Dominion-issue.

Then the carcass toppled and his blood ran cold an instant before it boiled with rage.

Pain lanced through Devon's leg, drawing him from the numbness of oblivion. He started to struggle, his left hand groping for another flash grenade, when his mind registered the quiet murmur that accompanied the poking and prodding that had brought him back to consciousness. From just above him and to the side he heard reassurances: "It is okay. You are safe now. Lie still while I tend your wounds."

Despite the too-regular vocal cadence—characteristic of robotic AIs—the words were soothing. He had read about the medical robots used by the Alliance in one of his tutorials, but never in his life had he expected to see one, let alone be in one's care.

"You are dehydrated. I am administering fluids."

"Devon... I am Devon," he muttered, then looked from the IV fed into his arm to the bag of fluids hanging off an upper strut on the robot and idly wondered what else was in that bag to make his head swim with just that slight motion. He couldn't bring himself to care through the pleasant numbness setting in. He did notice, though, that his right hand where the crab had clipped his thumb had already been bandaged. He muttered a thank you and tried to pat the robot to show his gratitude, but it gently extended a spare waldo and held him still as it continued to cut away his pant leg. Despite whatever was in the IV making him feel floaty, that hurt like hell.

To take his mind off the pain, Devon started talking. Randomly and about everything he had experienced in his short life. His granddad, his first girlfriend... when he was five, immigrating to Demeter, the terror of being thrown into battle with a gun that was little more than a club and a handful of grenades that just made noise, his concern for the woman who recorded the holochip around his neck, his last days on Earth, his conscription by the Dominion, he even spoke about his parents' death... something he'd not said a word about to anyone since the day they died.

He couldn't help it. The words tumbled from him like the guts that had spilled from the crab that cut him. He spoke until his words ran together and his head swam with the pain and the medication and the relief that he would not die beneath this rock, unremembered. And as Devon rambled, his gaze locked on the little blinking light beside the robot's optic. The flashes mesmerized him until his words trailed off and he barely noticed the robot's continued reassurances as it debrided his wound and stitched it up.

The entire time the medi-mech worked on the Dominion soldier wearing Justin's RF tags Rowland fought with himself. More than half a dozen times he started to key in the sequence that would override the treatment protocols and recall the 'mech—even after he learned the *kid* was just a conscript. He told himself that made no difference. Conscript or not, he had fought against Allied troops. He had taken up arms. Only by clinging to his healer's oath did Rowland resist. And then what the boy... *Devon* was saying sank in. Rowland could not ignore that the young woman the boy rambled about, the one he showed such compassion for, was Rowland's own sister.

Devon's words said it all... *'The Dominion screwed them both over.'*

...all of us, Rowland amended in his thoughts, and the hatred and rage toward this boy that had poisoned his heart ran out of him.

Feeling only sorrow for his sister and growing compassion for Devon, Rowland continued to stand vigil as the 'mech finished its ministration. While it stitched and cleansed and bandaged he kept his eyes on Devon's face and considered what would happen to the boy, conscript or not, if they were to send down a team to medivac him out. At best he would be "detained", at worse court-martialed for collusion. His forced service would dog him for the rest of his days, no matter where he went in Allied space. Any hope for a decent life would have died beneath that boulder.

Even with no clue who Devon was, Rowland's sister, Kelly, would be ashamed of him were he to allow that to happen. That wasn't the only reason James Rowland chose to do what was right—but it was the least complicated.

Though the boy needed to rest and recover, there wasn't time. Shortly, Allied forces would be moving in to resecure the area. Once that happened Devon would become yet another casualty of war. Rowland overrode the 'mech's protocols and took over the waldos. Keying in the sequence that loaded the built-in hypodermic with a high dose of adrenaline—such as would be administered to counteract heart failure in a patient—he injected half of it into Devon, then let the other half drain harmlessly onto the ground. As he waited for the injection to counteract the sedative that had finally taken effect, Rowland linked the camera on his terminal to the monitor inset on the 'mech. When the boy began to stir, Rowland cleared his throat to get his attention, then waited for Devon to regain his focus before he spoke.

"I am Major James Rowland, medical supervisor aboard the Allied transport *McCoy*. You—*Sergeant Krougliak*—just died," he said with a significant look. As he spoke, he manipulated the waldos once more, reaching out to lift the Allied tags—and his sister's holochip—from around Devon's neck. "You need to get out of there before the Alliance arrives."

Devon remained completely still, his expression equal parts fear, doubt, and confusion. "Why are you doing this?"

Rowland struggled a moment with how to answer. What he could say that this kid would understand, out of the confusing tangle of things that went into changing the outcome of this encounter?

"You aren't who we're out here fighting, son," he finally answered. "Now pull yourself together, lose the uniform, and de-ass that field, before the ground forces show up for clean-up duty. There's a town five klicks south of you, they can get you back to your settlement..." he stopped himself from finishing. The kid didn't need to know the town very well might no longer be there. "Go... find your way home and don't look back."

As he spoke, Rowland recalled the medi-mech and officially logged in Sergeant Justin Krougliak's time of death, unable to avoid breaking his sister's heart, but saving an innocent in the process.

The Devil's Own Luck

A Tale of the Kalderãs Clan

I LEFT THE KNIVES BEHIND. EVERYTHING I HAD LEFT IN MY LIFE HAS BEEN ripped away because I left the knives behind. Pain born of more than exile tore at Paolo's chest worse than the frantic clawing of lungs in a vacuum. He was sixteen and all alone in the universe. Too drained to resist such despair, he huddled in the little pocket of space he'd carved out in the center of the stacked cargo. Storage containers shielded him top, bottom, and sides as he gave in to the silent tears burning their way past his frozen soul. He leaned against the molded plastic crates, not caring if they shifted with his weight, halfheartedly wishing they would tumble, crushing his body as life had done his spirit. His sister would have scolded him.

How he wished by everything he'd once held sacred that she still could.

Terlinda's compressed ashes rested heavy against his heart. He tempted fate by keeping them close, but could not bring himself to let her go. The remnants of her physical self would surely draw her *mulò*—her ghost—to him. Would that be a blessing, or a curse? He could not say. All he knew was the black velvet pouch containing the cube of her remains wrapped in her favorite scarf served as the sole touchstone left to Paolo's life before he'd killed a man, sliced him from neck to nut sac with antique knives passed down in his family for generations. Knives as distinctly Romani as the nanite-infused tattoos scrolling every inch of Paolo's skin. Knives he had left buried deep in the corpse.

Might as well have signed his name.

None among the Kalderăs Clan held blame against him, but the Rom had a saying: *family before all others*. When a friendly dockmaster warned them that the military base on Xerxes had deployed forces in pursuit of the Caravan, Paolo slipped away at the next refueling station, determined to protect his remaining loved ones. He'd made it as far as the outpost orbiting Io before the grunts caught up with him. After that it had been one near miss after another.

Until now. This encounter could not yet be called a miss.

His bitter heart resisted anything even vaguely resembling prayer to any faith. Instead his thoughts maintained a silent litany: *I'm not here. I'm not here. I'm not here.* Though there seemed little reason to cling to life, of one thing he was certain... no one would claim justice on him for the righteous vengeance he had wrought. Tran did not deserve to be mourned. He did not deserve to be remembered, save as a warning to others.

Barely realized at first, Paolo's breathing increased, growing louder and more aggressive as he thought of the man who had brutalized and killed his sister. The sound filled the small space where Paolo hid until he worried it would filter out to the storage compartment beyond.

He buried his rage before it betrayed him. Slowing his heartbeat and muffling his breath, he curled his body into a compact ball as only a trained contortionist could, head nestled in the pocket formed of arms and tucked knees. *I'm not here. I'm not here. I'm not here.* Weary beyond bearing, Paolo lost himself in sleep's oblivion as the phrase repeated in his head.

The subtle sound of engines cycling down to dock woke him.

Crap! He couldn't believe he'd overslept. Instinct ordered him to scramble for his post before Terlinda gave him more grief about penalty fees for missing their scheduled docking window. It was her favorite gripe. Swearing beneath his breath lest she hear him, Paolo jerked, snapping out of the knot he'd huddled in. Or tried to, anyway.

A nova erupted in his head as the back of his skull thudded against something hard, and his foot—likewise striking an unyielding surface—stung with the impact. Immediately he curled back into a tight ball. *What the hell?* Where was he? Why wasn't he in his bunk? Drawing nearly spent air through clenched teeth, he resisted the urge to groan as he tried to fight past the pain. His lungs strained and more than sleep fogged his brain. It took him several long moments to realize what had happened. The reality he'd retreated from.

As he became more alert, Paolo examined the signs his subconscious had already interpreted. At some point during his ill-advised nap the crates he'd hidden among had been loaded on a ship going God-knew-where.

"*Mama dracului!*" Paolo hissed the curse in his native Romani, *the devil's mother.*

Tears stung his eyes and he found himself close to his limit. Ready to give up... to embrace his fate. The Clans had a word: *Prikàza.* It meant retribution visited on one who upset the spiritual balance. In other words, the Devil's own luck. With each misfortune that befell him, Paolo found it harder to believe he was not such a one, though he could not believe Terlinda's *mulò* responsible, as legends claimed.

Locking his jaw, he banished thoughts of ill luck, lest they invite more, and with tight, controlled motions, maneuvered in his hiding space until he crouched by the end he had staged as his exit. Had the placement shifted during loading? Was he even now trapped with no room to move the loose container out of his way? He had to try as his cocoon of air swiftly soured, each breath ending in a low, harsh cough. Taking care not to press against any other surface but the one that should be safe, Paolo cautiously pushed outward. A faint scrape froze him.

Slower. He must not draw attention if any were around to hear. That bright and shiny thought set off another wave of worry. Sound or silence, it wouldn't matter if his exit opened in plain sight. Gritting his teeth, he forced the concern away, not ready to allow fear to literally suffocate him. Again, he set his shoulder to the crate. Fraction of an inch by fraction of an inch, he edged it out from under the burden of its brothers. Even were he willing to shove his way out, it would not have been possible. It took all of his strength just to shift the container in these careful measures.

And suddenly, even his strength was not enough.

Paolo clenched his eyes tight and swallowed his panic. He forced himself to run his hand slowly along the surface of the crate in search of any detail that might reveal the issue. As his fingers reached the bottom edge he had the answer. He'd pushed the obstacle far enough that it had tilted infinitesimally, wedging the crate between the pallet it rested on and the container above. Paolo settled back on his heels and considered the matter.

If he pressed upward enough to free the edge he could destabilize the tower of crates, bringing them down on top of him. Shoving with more force until the one stuck came free could cause the same fate. If he waited, surely he'd expend the last of the air before anyone would chance to find him (such would be a typical *Prikàza*). But... if he shifted his pressure... like so... and nudged down and out on the tilted edge... *like so...*

The crate landed with a soft thud onto what he presumed was a cargo bay floor. Paolo braced for what seemed the inevitable, but the remaining stack did not, in fact, topple down on him. He drew several deep, shuddering breaths of fresher air into his lungs and grimly resisted the urge to drop prostrate in the space now sufficient to accommodate the length of him. He was not free of his unexpected prison yet, and even if he were, it courted danger to remain in the open. After resting a few moments he put his shoulder to the crate. Though both his lungs and his muscles burned, he once more pushed, this time in an effort to clear enough of a gap to crawl past the barrier. For a moment he feared himself trapped after all, but finally, with much straining, he created a gap just barely wide enough. Paolo silently thanked both his ancestors and carnival training equally as he contorted his muscles and turned his head, flattening sufficiently that he cleared the crates, losing no more that a layer or two of skin on either ear.

He slid his back along the top of the displaced crate and carefully drew out his legs until he moved free of the confinement. As he lay a moment in the near-dark, soundlessly catching his breath before he attempted to shove the crate back into place, he heard a noise; a hard *thunk* as of a hatch opening, followed by the sound of someone slowly clapping. An LED mega-cluster above his head came to instant life. Paolo tensed, his eyes squeezed closed against the sudden light. Spent, he wasn't quick enough to roll off of the crate. Before he could drop out of sight or reach, a firm grip pinned him in place.

"Consider me impressed," a man's gruff voice said from just above him. "For that matter, consider yourself impressed as well." A thick, calloused fist slammed into Paolo's jaw.

Paolo woke to jags of pain burning across various points of his body, but predominantly his jaw and his shoulders. The jaw was obvious. Being knocked senseless hadn't left him unable to remember how he'd gotten that way. But the shoulders... it took him a moment to figure that out. By the spread of his arms, it felt like someone had slid a roughly three-foot length of thick conduit across the base of his back and lashed his wrists around the ends, like a makeshift stock. Primitive, but damned effective.

There was little doubt, at this point, that the Fates had judged against him. Despair saturated his soul. He lay in the heap he'd been left in, head hanging, legs twisted, and back bowed. He didn't bother to look up at the sound of the hatch opening. In fact, he willed his body lax. Let them believe him still insensible. Nothing about his situation led him to expect this ship, or its crew, were upstanding or legal. Better to use this moment to observe and perhaps learn something he could turn to his favor.

By the distinctly different footsteps, Paolo knew three people had entered the chamber. Three men, he would guess by the heavy sound of each tread. Two moved to either side of him. Before he realized their intent, they had each gripped an end of his stock and hauled him up high until his feet dangled like a puppet. And still he forced his body to remain slack. The men just laughed and shook him until his arms screamed as he himself would not. Paolo resisted the urge to lash out with the legs they'd foolishly left unbound. He did send a silent command to the nanites beneath his skin to project the illusion of continued unconsciousness, though, before opening his eyes to study his captors.

Rough and prosperous were the first words he'd use to describe them. They appeared like standard space tramps, lean and hungry with banged-up gear, but each of them wore quality compression suits that gave lie to their overall impression. Their suits were void of any markings for rank or identification. Each of them had a utility pouch slung around their hips.

"Enough," the third man said with firm authority as he sauntered up to stand before them. He ran his hands over Paolo like a customer assessing goods in the market. "Bloody hell... a Gyp."

Paolo gritted his teeth at the racial slur, but continued pretending unconsciousness.

The leader's hand locked on Paolo's chin, gripping it hard. He forced Paolo's head back until they stared eye to eye, though only Paolo was aware of that. He catalogued the man's face: square, with a cleft chin and too-full lips, hard eyes and heavy brow. A thin, straight scar marred the left cheek, and another, more jagged example bisected his right eyebrow. His teeth were decent enough, but his breath foul. Paolo barely bothered noting the dark brown hair. It was too easily changed. But that face. Paolo would remember it. The Rom believed in vengeance nearly as much as luck, be it good or bad.

Oblivious to Paolo's true state, the leader went on. "No. Not worth keeping. Too big to crawl the conduits... too small to be of use for anything else that needs doing." Then the man tracked a finger over Paolo's tattooed face. "Besides, he's a Gypsy... definitely not worth the amount of trouble he'd be.

"We'll leave him with the rest of the marks," the leader continued. "Strip him of anything worth having and then get your asses back to the cargo bay. We have less than an hour to shift the goods over to the *Barbary* and disengage before this heap dives into the asteroid belt."

The man pivoted abruptly and headed for the hatch.

Something in his words triggered a memory. Faint, but insistent. Aside from the luxuries they offered, the Rom made great trade in information. A while back the Kalderäs Clan had learned of a band of pirates operating in fringe space, the areas past the edges of the more active trade routes. One of the known pirate vessels was the *Barbary*.

Paolo bared his teeth at the departing man's back, only to hiss in pain as his holders dropped him abruptly to the ground. Ingrained training had him remain relaxed as he fell. He didn't tense until the first booted foot took him beneath the ribs. Something cracked and he could not help but cry out. Pride cut the cry off and experience prompted Paolo to tense his muscles against the rest of the men's blows, but not to fight back. Understandably his illusion of unconsciousness fell away as his focus turned toward minimizing the beating. He did not let it go on for long, just enough to satisfy the thugs, before begging for mercy. They laughed and aimed a few more kicks, until their leader's voice sounded over the wall comm.

"Get your asses to the bay! Anything we're forced to leave behind comes out of your cut."

Paolo, struggling to breathe and startled by the sudden sound, lost focus on his tormentors. An unexpected kick connected forcefully with his already abused jaw. What color existed in the hold bled off leaving Paolo's vision briefly awash in shades of grey. He closed his eyes and fought not to be sick as his head bobbed uncontrollably. When rough hands began to paw among his clothing he attempted to kick out at them. The men laughed, the sound oddly muffled, as they slapped his feet away. He bucked and thrashed as they stripped him of what little he had left in the world, all but his clothes. But when one of them snatched the velvet pouch containing Terlinda's remains from around his neck Paolo raged and tried to ram him with the end of the conduit.

"Give her back! That's worth nothing to you!"

He knew he should have kept his mouth shut even as he spoke, but by then it was too late. With a smug sneer the pirate slid the pouch over his bald head in a blatant taunt. Paolo imprinted the man's face on his memory and lunged at him, but the other man yanked him back. Again, they laughed and one of them landed a punch in his gut. A shove sent him backward to the deck where the impact of his weight against the length of conduit felt as if it all but crushed his forearms. Before they could start beating him again, the wall comm squawked once more. Paolo recognized the leader's voice, though he could not make out the words past the agony buzzing through his brain. He lay in a haze as his assailants delivered parting blows, then left the chamber, harsh laughter trailing behind them.

It would be so easy to give in to his misery and fate, were it not so contrary to his Rom nature. Paolo instead focused on his pain. On compressing it. On shoving it deep into a mental hole where he could not feel it.

A lifetime of training returned his breath to slow, steady measures and his will forced each abused muscle to relax as he assessed his situation. Whatever the reason for his assailants' primitive measures, they worked to Paolo's favor. First he tested the bond around his wrists. He gritted his teeth as he flexed his hands and attempted to roll his wrists. It did not feel as though they'd bound him with rope or cord. It took effort, but he dropped his gaze and bent his body until he could just see the dull grey strips of duct tape that held him secure.

Paolo cursed. He did not have time to strip the tape, presuming there was even a surface to scrape it against. The leader had said they'd not quite an hour before the unpiloted craft entered the asteroid belt... and almost certain destruction.

About ten minutes had already passed. Paolo would have to work fast to free himself. Vengeance demanded it, as did the sheer cussedness of the Rom, which drove Paolo to preserve what life he had whether it seemed worth the living or not. At the end of everything, the Romani people were survivors. And even if Paolo were not confident of his own will to live, the leader of these rogues mentioned marks... victims. He would not stand by as more innocents like his sister were lost. The pirates were known for attacking colonizers, mostly automated ships sent out beyond settled space in search of inhabitable planets. That meant somewhere on this vessel as many as 160 people were ensconced in preservation tanks. The cargo the pirates stripped from the ship were the colonists' settlement supplies and what little personal goods they had paid to bring along. In other words, goods that meant the world to them. The Rom themselves had a history of picking pockets or fleecing the unwary, but seldom of robbing marks of their livelihood or *lives*.

Anger sent tension through Paolo's body. Tension was counterproductive to the task at hand. Closing his eyes and emptying his thoughts, Paolo instead focused on the muscles in his shoulders, arms, back, abdomen, and buttocks. With fine adjustments he worked them, stretching and contorting respectively, until slowly his hips and ass rested on the conduit, then slid backward over it. For a few moments, he allowed himself to rest, jaw clenched against the pain the familiar actions caused his abused flesh before he buried it deep once more. He sat with the conduit wedged beneath his thighs, arms stretched taut and head pounding. In his mind he heard Terlinda's voice muttering and kvetching: *No... no... No stopping in the middle. There will be time for resting when you've stopped the bastards.* Paolo could almost picture the outrage snapping in her dark, doe-like eyes and chuckled before he remembered. Outside of his thoughts, he would never hear her bossing him again. But she was right, figment or not. Those men had taken her from him all over again, stealing the last thing that mattered to Paolo, just as they threatened to do to the unsuspecting colonists.

He was not ashamed to admit that Terlinda mattered to him more, though he would gladly thwart the pirates in all the evil they planned. Taking his time in freeing himself would not get her back. With the memory of his sister driving him, Paolo manipulated his body, moving and contorting, stretching his back until there was room enough between himself and the conduit to allow his knees to pass. He then bent and tucked them against his chest and flattened his toes until they also pushed their way past the length of pipe, which along with his arms, now curled in front of him. For a brief instant Paolo laid there trembling, breath sawing past lungs that would not fill fully as damaged ribs painfully reminded him of their presence. Even so, triumph sang the length of his nerves at this small success. But he was not yet free.

Fighting to ignore the muscle aches and pain pricks in his arms, Paolo drew them up toward his face, shifting his shoulders until his right wrist came within reach of his mouth. The skin was puffy and red; his fingers tingled. He tried not to think of the passing minutes as he gnawed at the tape, desperate to find or create an edge that he could then strip away. All the while his experienced ears strained for subtle changes in the engine noises. Had the men fled to the other vessel yet? He did not believe so, as the ship's engine worked hard, as if burdened beyond standard specifications.

He could not let the thought distract him from his task. Biting and tearing, biting and tearing. With a deep-felt urgency, he tore his way through the tape, stopping only to spit as the fragments clung to his tongue, leaving a chemical residue that caused his mouth to water in protest, which interfered with his efforts. Finally, the last strands snapped. He nearly screamed as every nerve ending flared and pulsed with restored blood flow.

"*Căcat!*" *Shit!* Paolo bit off the curse as he shook the hand to restore sensation enough to free his other wrist. He lost some skin in his haste as he ripped the last of the tape away. Weary and aching, he wanted nothing more than to sink to the deck and let his body recover, but time would not allow it. He had thirty minutes left to save his ass and the ship with it.

And all he could think of was getting his sister back.

Paolo scrambled to his feet and staggered to the hatch, his body throbbing with the wasted effort. No matter how he worked the bolt, the way remained barred. The pirates had locked the compartment, showing an annoying bit of foresight. Gritting his teeth, Paolo turned to the wall comm. A standard-issue unit, it had basic system access: emergency alerts, ship-wide communications, climate controls for the compartment, and a bare-bones ship's schematic, enough to show someone where they were and how to get around through the corridors. Not enough to show Paolo the maintenance infrastructure, but it did identify the ship's class, which served just as well. A nomadic race dependent on spacecraft for their existence, the Rom made sure all in the Clan had a basic knowledge of existing ship design; how to identify them, fly them, and—if need be— disable them. Paolo himself had excelled beyond basic in all three regards. He easily recognized the ship as a Portmann- class colonizer. The Portmanns were an economical design, compact and frugal in regards to space. According to the schematic he was not far from the engine room. If he could get there, he could sabotage the engines before the ship nosedived among the asteroids.

Paolo searched the walls for a maintenance hatch. He discovered it in the corner of the room and nearly broke his vow to never again lift prayer to any god as he dropped to his knees, hands running frantically around the edge of the removable panel. A shuddering, relieved sigh sent sharp jags of pain through his abused torso as he found the pressure points that popped the panel away from the wall. Perhaps he wasn't quite as cursed as he feared... Paolo cut the thought off and made a sign against evil.

Such careless hope tempted the Fates to prove a man wrong.

He was about to duck through the hatch into the infrastructure of the ship when instinct drew his shoulders tight and made his belly burn. Memory of the strength and cruelty of his captors stopped him mid-crouch. Paolo turned and snatched up the conduit to which he'd been secured. It would make a serviceable club, if just a bit unwieldy.

At least nominally armed, he exited the compartment. He set the pipe down and pulled the hatch back into place behind him before picking up his makeshift weapon once more. Then he oriented himself, calling to mind the memory of the schematic and marrying it to his knowledge of the Portmann design. Paolo crouched and slipped in among the conduits and wires, contorting himself to pass among the infrastructure. He kept an eye to his left, watching for the reinforced bulkheads visible at regular intervals to mark the proper distance past the intervening compartments. When he judged he had gone far enough he turned left, and made his way through another tangle, before stopping by a full-sized maintenance hatch. If memory were correct, this brought him to a corridor that led to the engine room. Unfortunately, this was as far as the maintenance area extended. The heavily armored engine room was self-contained in case of catastrophic failure. From here he must venture into the open.

Not for the first time in his short life Paolo wished the holographic properties in his tattoos could be used to appear invisible. Such an illusion was beyond the capability of the nanites imbedded beneath his skin, however. Instead, he used his skills as a sneak—something every Rom learned almost before they could walk—to keep to the shadows created by the support struts that ran the length of the corridor at intervals.

Ten minutes had passed since he'd escaped when the corridor he traveled intersected with another. The sound of boots thudding on the deck came from his right. Paolo pressed himself into the shadow of the nearest strut. He stilled his breathing and visualized the nanites mimicking the wall behind him. Not the same as being invisible, but close, as long as he did not move. The footsteps came closer and Paolo could not completely silence the growl that rumbled in his throat as a familiar, bald-headed man entered the intersection. Terlinda's velvet pouch still hung around the pirate's neck.

Paolo struggled to remain motionless. Every nerve prickled with the need to snatch her away. His grip tightened on the length of conduit and he slowly eased his foot forward only to draw back as another voice called out from down the corridor at Paolo's back.

"Yo, Bock. What the hell are ya doin'? Cap's lookin' for ya. He's pissed."

Paolo squeezed his eyes closed and pressed tighter into his corner niche, his ears straining for any indication the man drew closer.

Bock stopped, casting an annoyed look over his shoulder. "Forgot somethin'. I'll be right there."

The slightest bit of tension eased from Paolo's shoulders. He could hear the footsteps fading as the other pirate walked away.

Bock grimaced. A hard light glimmered in his eye as he turned and continued the way he'd been heading. Paolo fought back the urge to cry out in frustration. The pirate moved in the opposite direction of the engine room. Paolo could follow the man. He could stalk in Bock's wake, waiting for a chance to reclaim the pouch containing his sister's remains, but would there still be time to stop the vessel from its ill-fated rendezvous with the asteroid belt?

Paolo sighed in frustration. His gut burned with the decision he knew had to be made. There were lives at stake and Terlinda would not have thanked him for putting the dead before the living. He couldn't go anywhere, however, until the way was clear. Creeping to the end of the corridor, he willed the nanites to mimic the floor, then dropped low to peer around the corner.

Bock had stopped in front of a compartment with *Cryo-Storage* stenciled beside the hatch. His manner and the way his gaze kept darting down the corridor spoke of the man's desire not to be caught. Paolo tensed as Bock opened the hatch and slid inside. Something in his expression echoed Paolo's memories of Tran.

Instinct sent Paolo to his feet and halfway to the cryo-storage compartment before the conscious decision had been made. As he walked, he called to mind every detail of the pirate captain's face... his clothes... the timber of his voice. Every nasty expression and unconscious mannerism. With each step, Paolo transformed a little more until he stood before the compartment as the perfect image of the man who'd condemned him. He slowly opened the hatch to the sight of Bock running his fingers over the surface of a preservation tank he prepared to extract. If not for the trans-alum glass the man's hand would have fondled the young girl encased inside. Fury lunged up from Paolo's belly in reaction, drawing his muscles taut and rolling his lips back in a snarl. The girl looked nothing like his sister, but wore Terlinda's face all the same, in Paolo's mind. His breathing sped up and his fingers tightened on the conduit he still carried. He must have made a noise because Bock pivoted around. Judging from the way the man's face paled the nanites must have translated Paolo's rage onto the pirate captain's expression.

"Aw, come on, Cap... can't we bring along just one? We could all use a soft berth to sink anchor in..."

Paolo growled and fought the violent impulses bombarding him. In the back of his thoughts a clock frantically ticked away the doomsday hour. There was no time for beating the bastard to a pulp. The desire must have translated to his expression, though.

Bock fell silent but did not move away from the preservation tank. He looked sullen, the set of his jaw rebellious as he shifted his stance into something more dangerous.

"She's mine, then," he insisted as he pivoted full around, body tense and aggressive. "My cut of the spoils... you can't argue against that, yeah?"

Paolo's gaze fixed on the pouch hung around the man's neck. His fingers ached to snatch it from the man's dead carcass. All it would take was a solid swing of the conduit to the side of Bock's bald head. It was an effort to resist, but Paolo had to if he and the unsuspecting colonists were to come out of this alive. He focused on channeling the pirate captain. Voices were trickier than physical appearance, but Paolo was a fair mimic.

"Get back to the *Barbary*, now," he ordered in Cap's voice. "Or I'll kill you myself and you'll have no share! We're running out of time."

Bock's features hardened and his eyes took on a hard gleam that did not bode well for Paolo. The pirate started forward, his hands fisting, when the comm engaged and the captain's voice crackled across the line.

"Bock, you have two minutes to get your ass on the *Barbary* or we're leaving you behind. We've got a military cruiser headed this way."

The captain's words triggered a violent pounding in Paolo's chest. A military cruiser? What were the chances it was tracking him? He couldn't figure out how, but clearly they had some way. Farfetched as it sounded, it began to look like his name had changed to *Prikàza*. On the bright and shiny side, his bad luck likely improved the colonists' and his own chances of survival. Of course, that last might have proved a bit too optimistic, judging from the way Bock looked at him.

The pirate's expression cycled from stunned to disbelieving and settled on enraged. As the man lunged forward, Paolo raised the length of conduit and swung it with all his might. The blow connected with Bock's shoulder and sent him careening into the bulkhead. The pirate caught himself and pushed back until he aimed at Paolo once more.

"I don't know how you did it, but you're dead, Gyp," Bock growled, making the only assumption he could.

Paolo laughed, his borrowed face set in grim lines. "I'm not that lucky," he said as he swung again, only to have the pirate grab the conduit. Before he could remove it from Paolo's grasp the ship jerked beneath their feet, likely jarred by the *Barbary's* ion wake as the pirate ship departed with haste. Or maybe they'd already entered the edges of the asteroid belt. Either way, the disruption sent both combatants to the deck in a heap, Paolo on top, smiling with satisfaction.

If there was anything the Rom knew it was how to fight dirty.

As the two of them tumbled, Paolo released his grip on the conduit and instead grabbed for the pouch hanging around

Bock's neck. He then yanked the man's head toward him as he sent his own slamming forward. Blood erupted from Bock's nose and his eyes rolled into his head. Paolo got his feet beneath him and fought the urge to twist the lanyard in his hands until Bock's face went blue. Breathing hard with the effort to resist, Paolo instead spat on the pirate.

"Well you're certainly not good enough for *my* sister!" he growled as he slipped Terlinda's remains over the unconscious man's head, before kicking him back to the deck. Paolo hung the pouch once more around his own neck and quickly secured Bock with duct tape from the pirate's utility pouch.

Biting back a groan of pain from his earlier beating, Paolo struggled to control his breath. He lost himself a moment as his eyes locked on the young girl in her preservation tank. So like his sister... and yet so not like her. Something healed within his heart at knowing he had kept this one safe.

The jarring, raucous sound of a proximity alarm broke Paolo from his musing. He lunged for the wall comm by the compartment hatch and called up the ship's alert system. He cursed at what he saw.

There wasn't time to stop the vessel from entering the asteroid belt. Fortunately, the Portmann class had decent hull shielding—more than capable of absorbing blows from the dust, pebbles, and head-sized rocks that mostly made up an asteroid belt—and it was equipped with auto cannons that could take care of the bigger bits, as long as someone was at the helm to steer around anything the size of a shuttle craft or larger. Paolo swallowed hard as acid scored his throat. Their only hope now lay in *him* navigating a path through that relentlessly tumbling obstacle course. He was better than good as a pilot, but navigating an asteroid belt alone was a tricky proposition.

As he ran for the command deck, Paolo gripped Terlinda's remains and prayed for all he was worth.

No Man Left Behind

an Alliance Archives Adventure

SERGEANT JUSTIN KROUGLIAK OF THE 428TH RECON WOKE WITH A start, confused as someone delivered a powerful kick to the cot he lay on. If not for the pong of drying blood surrounding him, he would have expected he was late for PT or duty. He opened his eyes and struggled to sit up. Immediately, he noticed a Dominion officer staring down at him with icy blue eyes brimming with hatred. (The man wore no rank, but the uniform and posture were unmistakable.) The second thing Justin noticed was that his own uniform was covered in blood—mostly, from what he could tell, someone else's. The third thing he noticed— and the most troubling—was that his radio-frequency tags were missing from around his neck.

Justin fell back on the cot and just stared up at the enemy, saying nothing.

The officer pivoted and walked out, calling back to two soldiers Justin hadn't noticed until now, "Bring him."

He didn't resist, but he didn't exactly cooperate, as they came to either side of the cot, gripped him by the upper arms, and hauled him to his feet. Justin's head swam and if not for their rough hold on him he would have fallen. Maybe more of the blood was his than he'd thought. He struggled to regain his balance as they marched him from the cell, having no doubt they would drag him otherwise. They led him outside and across a barren compound to a Quonset hut that seemed to serve as temporary command of the makeshift camp. Though the bright sunlight caused his head to pound violently, Justin forced his eyes to stay open, doing his best to scan the terrain without seeming to. Not that the grunts hauling him around paid any attention. Other than the blockhouse they held him in and the hut, there were no permanent structures. There were, however, plenty of soldiers bivouacked beneath the towering old-growth trees. He nearly slumped in relief. Not at the soldiers, but at the landscape. It appeared they were still on Demeter. One point in his favor, anyway. If he could just disappear up into the canopy...

Memories began to surface. He and the 428th had been securing a new sector. Coop was running Treybot, their bomb-detection robot, with the rest of the unit following behind, dealing with any explosive ordnance discovered. As they cleared the treeline, they encountered a company of Alliance infantry pinned down by the enemy. The last thing he remembered... well, that would be the last thing he remembered.

They must have joined the fight and, clearly, it hadn't gone in their favor... or at least not in his. He had to assume some soldier had stripped him of his RF tags when they'd snatched him from the battlefield. The absence of their slight mass resting against his chest weighed heavy on him. With those tags and the right codes, the enemy could learn pretty much anything about him. Nothing critical, just his personal details. Given time they could learn more if they had resources inside Alliance territory. But nothing right now. Nothing that would endanger his unit.

How had they faired...? He shut down that line of thought fast. He couldn't think about Coop and the others. They were either out there or they weren't. He chose to believe they were, but he couldn't depend on it and worrying would only mess with his head. With deep, centering breaths, he shut down his emotions and focused on the shit-basket he was currently in now... and how to get out of it.

The guards let him trip over the doorframe he wasn't paying attention to. Justin kept his expression carefully neutral and picked himself back up, standing at attention (out of habit) and seemingly staring at nothing as he assessed the room: A desk, a single chair (occupied by the officer from earlier), and nothing else. No help there. The guards remained outside, but a medic filed in and started laying out his kit on the desk: bandages, tear-tape, alcohol swabs, liquid sutures, a white transdermal pain patch. That's it, nothing usable there—though the pain patch was a surprise. They must have plans if they were wasting that on him.

"If you would sit on the edge of the desk," the medic instructed him, his tone businesslike and impersonal. Without hesitation, Justin complied. He didn't know why they wanted to patch him up, but he sure as hell wasn't going to miss the opportunity to improve his chances at getting free. Justin watched closely as the guy treated his wounds. He frowned.

There was a ring on the medic's finger. A simple, silver-tone band. Flat and kind of thick. A wedding band? That's what it looked like. Most soldiers—on either side—abstained from such open signs of attachment. Why hand the enemy a tool to use against you? Anything was a source of intel during wartime. Of course, he could be conscripted. Justin kind of envied the guy, his own finger never felt so bare as it did now. A fleeting image of his wife Kelly rose in his memory, wearing her trademark smirk and her flight gear.

Again, he shut down his emotions, hard.

Justin watched closely as the guy treated his wounds. Motions quick and confident, but relaxed, as if he was just another patient, not an enemy soldier. The guy was good. Efficient. Not too rough, though there was a time or two before the pain patch kicked in where Justin couldn't help but hiss. When the medic was done, he rested his hand on Justin's wrist, the cool metal of the ring pressed against his skin. Justin started to tense and pull away, feeling a faint prick as the medic tightened his hold.

Something wasn't right. Justin's breath came faster as his body tingled. Every impulse shouted at him to get clear, to break the medic's grip. By then, of course, it was too late. He didn't know what they'd done but his blood began to burn and every muscle in his body went stiff and unresponsive. If he could have, he would have screamed. All he managed was a grimace and he'd had to fight to manage that. A memory surfaced from his childhood of his mother warning him not to make faces: *If you're not careful, it will freeze that way.*

What do you know? Justin thought. *Mom was right.* Silently, he laughed, but even in his mind there was an edge to it. He knew when he was fucked.

The medic quickly stepped back, his hands falling to his side. Justin met his gaze and saw regret reflected back before the man looked away. With haste, the medic packed up his kit and left. For untold agonizing moments, Justin and his captor sat in silence. Justin had no idea how long, but his need to scream in rage increased exponentially. His grimace slowly shifted into a snarl as the muscles of his face relaxed. Or fell back under his control, at least.

"If we wanted to kill you," the officer said in a cold matter-of-fact tone, "we could have done so on the battlefield, Sergeant Krougliak. But let's just say we're reserving that option for now."

He pulled open one of the desk drawers and tossed a new uniform in Justin's direction. Then he took something else out. Justin couldn't move his head to see what it was but then he didn't have to. The officer stood and walked around the desk to stand in front of him. In his one hand were Justin's name tape, rank marker, and unit patch. In the other was a circular object.

"Your demolition skills are useful to me," the officer said as he held up the patches, "but I am not a fool." He then held up the object, a metal band much like the ring the medic had worn, only larger. Bracelet-sized, large enough to fit a man. Knowing what was coming, Justin struggled to move. His jaw clenched and his fingers twitched, but the rest of his body betrayed him as the Dominion officer secured the manacle snug around Justin's wrist. He had regained enough sensation to feel the tiny pinpoints just touching his skin. "You've had a small taste of the neurotoxin from Corpsman Pierce's ring... just enough to appreciate the severity of its effects. This..." The officer tapped the metal band. "This will kill you outright; don't give me a reason to activate it.

"I'm through losing men and territory because of Allied soldiers. You work for me now, Sergeant. Krougliak... or for your life... however you care to think of it. Once you can move, change. My men will escort you back to your new quarters."

The medic showed up the next morning before dawn to change Justin's bandages. He looked like he wanted to say something, but all he murmured was, "I am Anatoliy, I did not enlist."

The man had a faint Czech accent that reminded Justin of Děda... his grandpa. Taking a calculated risk, he responded "Ano," 'yes' in the man's language. Anatoliy's eyes widened, but he said nothing more, his shoulders tense. As he worked, he seemed almost poised to speak, then his eyes would dart toward the door and his lips would press thin again. Justin remained patient and cooperative. What choice did he have?

Just before he left, the medic seemed to make up his mind. He leaned in close and, barely moving his lips, he whispered in Czech, "The lieutenant, he lost his younger brother to an Allied mine. It would not take much to convince him to set that off." Anatoliy dipped his head toward the manacle, though there really was no need. Justin nodded as the man hurried from his cell.

Lieutenant, huh? Justin filed the information away. None of the Dominion soldiers wore any markings he could identify. Safer in a war zone, he supposed, but not very convenient for him. And that is when it hit him. *He* no longer wore identifying marks and his RF tags were gone. As far as the Alliance was concerned, he was another faceless Dominion soldier.

And Sergeant Justin Krougliak was dead.

Which meant Sergeant Justin Krougliak was on his own.

The rest of Justin's day, along with the next and who knew how many more after that, disappeared into a fog of exhaustion as he went from one shit job to another around the camp. They worked him hard and long and watched him closely. For everything from shitting to shaving to slaving, some Dominion grunt was his shadow. The only time there wasn't someone standing over him was when he slept and even then, he was sure someone stood outside the door.

So far, he hadn't done a thing with his demolition skills but the lieutenant's words ricocheted around Justin's thoughts any time the fog cleared. What would he be asked to do against his own forces? Against innocent civilians caught between their two armies? And how could he avoid it? The only way he could think of was to refuse and take his poison. After all, the Alliance already thought he was dead… which meant Kelly had been informed he was dead. What did his life matter if he couldn't get back to her?

He clenched his teeth and mentally kicked his own ass. Rising from his bunk he ignored the throb of his injuries—joined by a few new ones—and dropped to the floor in a set of punishing pushups, gritting through the pain. The transdermal patch had long ago lost its effectiveness and not been replaced. It had done its job, snare to their trap. Fucking thing should have set off a red flag. Like the Dominion ever did anything benevolent toward an Allied soldier. On each upward stroke of the pushup, Justin held the position for a count of five before lowering down and holding for another count of five. His muscles screamed but did their job, just like he would, if not in the way the Dominion expected. His wife was a bad-ass fighter pilot, one of AeroCom's legendary Morrigans, she would kick his ass herself if she could hear his thoughts, if she even suspected he'd given up hope of getting back to her.

When his body began to quiver, Justin lowered himself to the cool concrete of the floor. It felt good but what he needed now was some sleep. Without rest, he would be useless to react when his opportunity presented itself. Rest was the difference between life and death on the battlefield. He was getting back to his wife. He climbed to his feet and lay down on the cot, barely more comfortable than the floor had been. No matter what the Dominion put him through, he planned to be ready to take the fight to the enemy.

Within moments he drifted off as any seasoned soldier could, no matter the conditions.

Justin came awake instantly as the door to his cell slammed open. He leapt from his cot just moments before the guard flipped it over, nearly crashing it into his legs. He held himself very still, not showing any aggression, but more than ready to evade, for whatever good it would do him. From the open doorway, where he stood limned in moonlight, the lieutenant spoke, "Time to earn that air you're breathing, Sergeant. Krougliak." The tone of his voice was akin to a death knell. Something happened. Something bad. And Justin expected he wasn't the only one going to pay for it.

One of the guards thrust a helmet and basic tactical gear at him. They waited as he suited up, then marched him from the blockhouse what had to be only hours since he'd lain down to sleep. He followed them to the command hut, bypassing the entrance to the lieutenant's office and circling around to the back side where an open door led to a munitions bunker. Three men waited inside in full oobleck—or liquid Kevlar—body armor with night-vision gear perched on their helmets. Four demolitions kits sat at their feet.

"Meet your new team. You don't need to know anyone's name," the officer said, before pausing and pointing at the massive soldier in the middle. "Well, except for his. We're calling him 'Kill Switch' for now."

Justin hardly heard the words, his eyes locked on those kits. Knowing they meant only one thing. Then what the lieutenant said sank in and Justin's gaze lifted to the man before him, center of the pack. He kept his expression neutral and hooded his eyes. The significance of the man's handle wasn't lost on Justin, even without the soldier's evil leer. Kill Switch lifted his hand in a mocking salute, baring a metal band on his wrist similar to Justin's, only one with a clear pressure switch on the exterior.

One of Justin's guards gave him a shove toward the men. Without a word, he shouldered one of the kits and waited for the others to do the same. All the while, his mind worked furiously to find a way out of this circle of hell.

As the four-man unit headed for the forest past the soldiers' tents, a form rose from the nearest one. The Dominion soldiers went on alert, but relaxed as the man spoke with Anatoliy's soft tones, "Wait, allow me to check his injuries before you go, so he does not slow you."

Kill Switch's eyes narrowed until the whites were but a sliver as he looked from the medic to Justin and back again. He gave an abrupt nod. The medic ducked back into his tent and came out with his kit, quickly and efficiently going about his task before the soldiers could change their mind. Old bandages came off and the wounds were cleaned before new went on. While he worked, he avoided Justin's eyes but kept up a steady murmur of Czech words too low for anyone beyond their immediate sphere to pick up. "This is all I can do for you now..." the medic said as slid a length of tempered steel into Justin's boot under the cover of darkness. Then he pressed a clear transdermal patch on Justin's wrist right above the manacle. Justin snarled and started to draw back as the skin grew warm and began to tingle in an almost familiar way, but not quite. Anatoliy risked looking up for a fleeting moment and just barely shook his head. "It is a ruse," he said, his fingers settled on the patch and trailed over the metal band as he drew away. "Remember... it is a ruse." And then the man was gone before the soldiers could order him away.

Justin watched the medic duck back into his tent. Dare he trust him? This wasn't the first time Anatoliy had warned him, but his words conflicted, then from now. Had he truly understood the man's hushed whispers? Which was the truth? Justin was still conflicted when Kill Switch grabbed him roughly by the arm and yanked him into motion. That decided him. There was only one group these ordnance packs could be intended for and Justin would be damned before he helped make that happen. Either Anatoliy told the truth or Justin would die. Either way, he was out of here.

As they made their way through 'undergrowth' taller than most Terran forests, Justin stumbled with the grace of a lumbering bear while the others moved like jaguars through the grass. Of course, they wore night-vision goggles. He had to feel his way in the dark. After about an hour's march, they cleared the treeline and paused at the edge of a war-torn field.

At this distance, in the faint moonlight, it was difficult to tell the terrain from the bodies.

Bile crept up Justin's throat. His jaw and every other muscle clenched. This wasn't the battle he'd been taken in. Too much time had passed. But it might well have been. So many lives sacrificed to the Dominion invasion. And they had the gall to blame the Alliance for their losses.

A hand reached out and yanked Justin down into a huddle.

Kill Switch glared at him. The promise in his expression one of death. The soldier's gaze then traveled to each of his men, clearly making sure all of them paid attention as he pulled open his kit and extracted the contents.

"Deploy the hydras in the open spaces where the enemy forces are likely to transit. The claymores place beneath the bodies." Here his gaze locked back on Justin, his expression one of venomous satisfaction. "Allied wounded first; carcasses second. Make them pay in blood and body parts."

Outwardly, Justin refused to react. Inside, his blood boiled and all he could picture was plunging the knife hidden in his boot deep in the man's eye socket.

These weren't just random Allied forces that would fall to the Dominion traps. Recon would be sent in first to clear the field for the medics. Very likely Justin's own unit, the 428th. What if they missed one of Kill Switch's little surprises? There was a reason the Dominion forces were called Demons by the Allied troupes. This was a new low even for them.

The unit leader repacked his kit with efficiency, then turned and motioned each of his men in a different direction, all but Justin. The two of them watched as they scurried off to wreak their havoc. Kill Switch then turned and shoved Justin ahead of him into the unassigned zone.

"You're with me, sunshine."

Justin tamped down his rage. He scanned the field, calculating the distance between the other men and their location. Then their location and the treeline. Could he make it? His fingers itched to grip Anatoliy's blade, but the odds were not yet in his favor. He had to wait until the others had begun their reprehensible efforts.

Kill Switch yanked him to a stop beside a crumpled mount in an Allied uniform. Justin looked down into a face way too young to be bathed in blood and battle grime. The kid's eyes fluttered briefly as his head rolled fitfully from side to side, but he didn't wake.

"Get cracking, you know what to do," Kill Switch ordered.

Sonofabitch! Justin's right hand flexed. That kid's momma didn't deserve to receive a letter from his CO. Not like this. Not ever. But definitely not like this. When Kill Switch shoved him to the ground Justin reached into his boot and pivoted, bringing his arm up in a single, fluid motion only to have the Dominion soldier block with a solid grip to Justin's wrist.

Rather than resist, Justin pushed into the hold, bearing the Demon to the ground. Any moment he expected a bullet to the brain as they grappled, but if the other soldiers noticed they didn't interfere. He twisted his arm and tried to use his momentum to drive the blade into his opponent, but Kill Switch rolled and thrust Justin away as they both scrambled to their feet.

Silently they circled one another, Justin trying not to trample the wounded kid, but Kill Switch didn't bother. Justin lunged and shoved the Dominion soldier away, reversing his thrust to swipe with his blade. The tip of his knife scraped over the liquid Kevlar and just nicked the edge of the soldier's wrist, drawing a single drop of blood.

Kill Switch bared his teeth and continued to circle, his eyes taking on an unholy gleam. The metal bands at each of their wrists glowed faintly in the twilight but the soldier didn't reach for his. Instead, he drew his own blade. For some reason, the man wanted this fight. He wanted it bad. And he wanted it personal.

Justin met his steady gaze and that is when it clicked. Icy blue eyes stared back at him brimming with both rage and hatred. Then he remembered what Anatoliy had told him way back that second day of captivity: The lieutenant, he lost his younger brother to an Allied mine.

Well... this guy was clearly related. But Justin had to wonder who they lost this time because this was a whole other level of escalation.

He heard a sound. The other soldiers converging? Or something closer? Justin dared not take his attention away from Kill Switch long enough to figure it out. They continued to circle and feign. Then suddenly the Dominion soldier stumbled and looked down. The kid... the wounded soldier, he'd feebly reached out and grabbed Kill Switch's leg throwing him off balance. In that instant of distraction, Justin lunged forward, his knife aimed just below the ribcage and angled for an upward thrust. His weight and momentum pressed it up into his opponent's chest to the guard.

As they fell to the ground, Kill Switch sneered and slammed his wrist against his armored thigh.

Justin tensed as the light slowly went out of his adversary's eyes.

For a moment nothing happened, then the skin beneath the patch on Justin's wrist began to tingle and his muscles locked up. His whole body burned with betrayal as the toxin took hold. It didn't matter that he was prepared to take this particular bullet by his own choice. He'd gambled, wanting to believe in Anatoliy. Allowed himself to hold hope in seeing Kelly once more. Not in this lifetime.

His only satisfaction now was that he'd taken Kill Switch with him.

Faintly, he heard the other men yelling, and even fainter yet, he heard approaching transports. Dominion or Alliance? It made little difference now...

He lay there collapsed atop the Dominion soldier's corpse. He couldn't move. And then he couldn't breathe. He barely felt it as the rest of the unit pounded up and rolled him away to retrieve their leader's body, leaving Justin in the dirt to stare upward as dawn lightened the sky.

Until his heart stopped. His back arched off the ground as that last muscle seized.

Then his world went black.

Sergeant Justin Krougliak of the 428th Recon woke with a start, confused as someone delivered a kick to the bottom of his boot.

"Wake up, Sleeping Beauty!"

He opened his eyes and struggled to sit up. The first thing he noticed was an Allied sergeant staring down at him. The second thing he noticed was the big-ass grin on Coop's face. The third thing he noticed—and the most perplexing—was he was still alive.

He didn't know how, but he was still alive.

Coop gripped him by the forearm, hauling him to his feet and right into a bear-hug. "Aren't you out of uniform, soldier?"

"Don't tell my wife..."

The whole unit laughed as they piled on to hug and slap his back, one of their own returned from the dead.

As he shook and laughed and delivered a few half-hearted punches at his team as they ribbed him, Anatoliy's words came back to him: *Remember... it's just a ruse.*

New Discoveries

A Story of Fremont

Two hours before dawn Sala's pillow shook violently, accompanied by a faint buzzing sound barely loud enough to rouse just her. In truth, she had lain awake most of the night, waiting with anticipation for the time just before the guards changed shifts. In slow, sliding motions she'd practiced for weeks, she reached beneath the pillow to shut off the alarm before it could disturb her parents. As she drew her hand out she snagged the pouch she had hidden in her bed last night. It held a flask of water, nutrient bars, a med kit, and a collapsible bowl, along with its more precious cargo of specimen bags, graphite pencils, and parchment. Scraps and cast-offs mostly, but she cherished them. The scientists at Artistos, Fremont's one city, would have used tablets to record data, which was all well and good, but her grandpa had taught her the joy of documenting specimens with careful strokes on paper she held in her own hands. Besides, she never would have been able to sneak off with the tech unnoticed.

Sliding from her cot to the floor with utmost care, she held her breath lest she draw the next one sharp and loud and disturb those she wished to leave sleeping. As she crept from the wagon she trembled, still awed by the uncommon ease with which she now moved.

She had been born with legs twisted and barely controlled, muscles and tendons drawn too short and tight. At Artistos, the colony doctors had corrected them the best they could, but certain things had been beyond them by the time she had been born. While she had grown able to walk, her gait proved awkward and rolling, not to mention painful.

Now, thanks to *them*—the *altered* that came to Fremont less than a year ago claiming the planet as their own, supposedly all legal and binding and not meaning squat, or so her Papa said—Sala's legs were as straight and smooth and able to move as if they'd never been twisted up, even if it had taken her six months to learn how to use them proper. Long, long months, but nothing compared to the almost twelve years she'd spent hobbled, watching others move freely, playing and exploring, *discovering* new things while she stayed at camp helping to catalog those things she longed to see first-hand.

Now... *now* she would explore the world she loved for herself. Not in the bits and pieces brought back to camp. Not from the safe conveyance of a wagon or lofted by a harness on her older brother's back as he hiked the wilds. As much as she appreciated Joram's willingness to do that for her, it just wasn't enough to observe. This... this was her chance to *live*... to discover new things first hand. For that alone she reveled in the transformation of her body. And yet it would be a lie to say all was now well for her. Sala had grown used to being stared at with pity, but the looks most other Roamers gave her had begun to change, ranging from uncomfortable to awed to cold and mistrustful.

Sala hardly cared what any of them thought, or so she told herself. There had already been looks before she was changed, so what if there were looks after? Her freedom was worth tolerating the attention, however uncomfortable. Determination firmed her features as she wended her way through the camp with quiet practiced motions, scrunching down small and pausing absolutely still wherever she hid as those ending their watch handed off their duties to those just coming on. Once they settled she resumed her slow, careful trek, keeping to the deep shadows of the wagons or terrain until she reached the brush surrounding the camp.

Excitement tingled across every nerve like the current that built in the air before an electrical storm as she stood at the edge of the hebra pens, murmuring soft, soothing noises to calm them before they betrayed her. Faint tremors went through her and anticipation clenched her belly as she stared out at the brush.

She had never been beyond the camp on her own.

Clutching her pouch, her gaze darted all around her in the faint pre-dawn light. A smile warmed her face and tears pressed against her eyes as she stepped away from the enclosure into the trees mentally cataloging things as she passed them. Pongaberries, just ripe and ready for picking, if only she could climb that high. Twintrees. Redberry bushes—also heavy with fruit. Ferns and sawgrass, creepers and nettles. So many species of plants she had never seen up close, only in sketches or as loose leaves or berries or twigs.

There wasn't much in the way of wildlife about. Likely a good thing, as her movements weren't that swift, but there were plenty of insects, with which she was already familiar. Still... to see them in the wild... Almost, she lost herself as she watched a fire wasp industriously gather tiny globes of dew to take back to its nest. Shaking herself from the wonder of her observation, Sala strove to remember how near she stood by the camp. To stay here was to risk discovery and the end of her first unsupervised excursion.

Continuing on her way through the brush, she headed for the perimeter, inside the sensors—if only just—but enough outside of camp that the landscape and wildlife remained mostly undisturbed. For a while she just wandered, taking care to avoid tripvines and sawgrass as she scanned for any plant or beastie she didn't recognize from her cataloging efforts. Mostly, though, she just enjoyed her new freedom of movement. Not just the ease of taking a step, but doing so without pain or fear she would overbalance and fall. And without others hovering nearby, trying to appear they weren't, just in case she tumbled.

All too soon she grew winded and her legs began to ache. She found a somewhat comfortable spot beneath a twintree and carefully lowered herself to the ground. For a time she just sat there, enjoying the song of Fremont as the night insects wound down to their rest and the birds began to stir and sing their morning song. Sighing with contentment, Sala drank from her flask and nibbled an energy bar, then took out her parchment and pencil nub. With a care and attention to detail learned at

Grandpa's side she drew and documented the area surrounding her. Sawgrass and ferns and flowers, mostly, with the occasional insect clinging to a blade of grass. All familiar, common elements that had surrounded her all her life, or recent finds she had helped catalog after someone else's discovery, but she cherished her first opportunity to observe them closely in their natural environ. While she longed to discover something new, for now she contented herself with studying nature and practicing the observation skills she would need when she did find that unique discovery, which she *would* find one day.

Sala focused so completely on her work that she barely realized how bright the morning grew or how long she had been out, until a rustling in the brush nearby startled her. She jerked her head up as her pencil point veered across her drawing, cutting a sharp line over a flower she had been delicately shading. A few yards beyond the perimeter sensors a cluster of ferns swayed where before they had been still. Sala peered closely but could not see what had disturbed them.

The birds around her had fallen silent.

A shiver skated across her shoulders. She remained within the perimeter, but as far as she could be from the encampment—and any help the others could offer. It had been unwise to lose track of herself like this. The morning grew late. If she strained she could make out the sounds of the camp waking. She gathered her things and pushed herself up from where she sat, bracing against the tree. As she hurried back as best she could she heard more rustling behind her and could not help but look behind her, fearing to see a pawcat or demon dog tracking her. She frowned. She saw no sign of those predators, but... but she would almost swear she saw a person disappear into the brush.

Sala did not bother with silence as she returned to camp. Instead she reached into her satchel for the collapsible bowl, stopping beside the redberry bush to harvest the ripe fruit. Surely Mama would not protest the treat, or think to question what else Sala may have been up to so early once she presented it to her.

"Good morning. Look what I brought," she said as she approached her mother, who appeared to be packing.

"Hurry, we're breaking camp. Akashi wants to be out of here within the hour."

Sala didn't dare frown, but her good cheer drained away. This was a settled camp, meant for a prolonged stay. That gave her more range of freedom. If they resumed roaming she would have a better chance at finding something new, but less likelihood of being able to sneak away to do so. She couldn't help it. Her lips turned down and her breath hitched just a little. Mother looked up sharply but said nothing.

"Come, Sala," she heard Papa call from the door of their wagon. "Eat this, then go help the catalogers secure the specimens."

His expression tightened as she drew near, his eyes shadowed, but then he smiled as she reached him and tousled her hair. Her papa loved her, but he was not happy it had taken the *altered* to help her. Only Mama's pleading and a long conversation with Akashi convinced him it was the only choice. Still, there were times he seemed guarded, as if he suspected more than her legs had been changed.

That was silly. Wasn't it? She would know. Wouldn't she?

Not liking those thoughts, Sala smiled an anxious smile up at Papa and hugged herself close to him. She didn't relax until his arms came around her and hugged back. The moment was fleeting, though. After just a few seconds he patted her shoulder and gently pushed her away.

"Here, now. We don't have much time."

Sala nodded and took the nutrient bar from him. She obediently nibbled at the edges. It sat heavy in her gut, along with the one she'd eaten earlier, as she headed for the research wagon.

No one told Sala the reason they had left their camp. Ultimately, they didn't have to. Even among the Roamers, idle gossip was a thing, and what tongue wouldn't waggle over the rumor of *altered* prowling around the wilds? The little Sala overheard made no sense. The kindest merely called the newcomers unnatural; those who spoke with more anger swore they were monsters and that they meant the settlers harm. More than one claimed they intended to steal the planet. That made no sense to

Sala. How did one steal a planet? Fremont had more than enough room for them all. Besides, the *altered* had been kind to her and made her better. Why do that if they only meant to hurt everyone?

And yet, Sala felt doubt darken her thoughts. She could tell her parents worried, and even Akashi—the most calm and accepting of anyone she knew—had ordered them to break camp. Reportedly, the guards had found tracks just outside the perimeter. Human tracks, or mostly.

Sala thought of the rustling she'd heard in the underbrush the day they had broken camp and shivered.

"Everything okay, sweetie?"

She looked up at her mother, her eyes wide, certain worry bled through her expression.

"Sala?"

"Sorry, Mama. I was just... do you think they're following us?" She said 'us', but she thought 'me'.

Mama frowned and her gaze darted toward the edges of their current camp, where Fremont's wild loomed, more than sufficient to hide both man and beast. "Don't be silly. Why would they?"

Sala had no answer for her. She didn't know. But even if she had, what could she say that wouldn't sound preposterous?

She rested her head against her mother briefly, then went back to sketching the latest batch of specimens, new variations of old finds. The subtle differences both fascinated and frustrated her. Oh, how she wanted to discover something new...

The next morning the Roamers resumed roaming. Sala sat beside her father on the driver's bench of their wagon and tried not to think about the *altered*. Instead she watched the hebras straining to pull the wagons up the tail end of the Eastern Trail, breaking off to follow what Sala called the Crooked Back Path, for the bumpy way it followed the edge of the mountain. She pictured it like the spine of a giant lying on his side and told herself tales about his long journey as she clutched tight to the bench in an effort to stay put. The hebras found this route difficult and even the camp dogs struggled to keep up, but

Mama explained the need to break their routine in case they *were* being followed. And so they continued for about a week until they reached a new camp between the river and the cliffs, one they had not used before, having only discovered it at the end of the last season on their way back to Artistos.

Sala twitched with excitement as they drew up to the not-quite cavern. She could picture the nearby river overflowing its bounds each rainy season for millennia, rolling and raging against the cliff that towered over it, never managing more than to carve away at its toes. Or so she imagined.

Whatever the cause, something had worn away the cliff face until it formed a deep, scooped-out pocket, the opening twelve feet high at the mouth and angling down toward the back until even Sala could reach up and touch the worn rock without stretching. All the wagons nestled nicely, if a bit closely, in the space, which offered protection on all but one facing. At the back a proper cave, small and dark, led deep into the cliff. The children—particularly Sala—were forbidden to explore it, but she knew some of the others already had.

Let them. She couldn't care less about a dank, dark hole.

She turned and faced the thriving wilderness, her gaze intent. The plants and bugs and beasties... They waited for her, along with all manner of opportunities to find something new and wondrous. Her eager grin twisted into a grimace. All of it out there... and there was next to no hope of her exploring. The tension had only grown as signs of trespass had been discovered *within* the perimeter sensors at the last nightly camp, with no alarm sounded. The guards continued to amplify security, to say the least.

Sala jumped as a hand came to rest on her shoulder, her thoughts still firmly on intruders.

"Whoa..."

Her muscles loosened as she looked up at Joram. He was ten years older than her and towered overhead as much as Papa did, if not more. Of course, she was tiny—just over four feet tall, thanks to how she had been born—so even those her own age stood over her, when they bothered to be near her at all.

As if privy to her thoughts, Joram knelt down. His arm settled around her waist. She leaned into his comforting presence.

"I have to go report in," he said softly, "but we could go exploring after..."

Oh how Sala wanted to say yes, but Joram was a scout. She knew reporting would not be quick. She turned her head to look at him. Weariness had etched faint creases around his eyes and drew down on the corners of his mouth, despite his ready smile. How she loved her brother, more inclined than anyone else in her life to figure out how to make her wishes happen rather than point out why they weren't possible. He never dwelled on her differences, had never counted them against her, not even out of concern, like their parents had in their efforts to protect her. For that reason she would not impose on him now. She leaned her forehead against his. Playfully, she wrinkled her nose. "Maybe a swim would be better... you're kind of stinky."

Her brother retaliated with tickles until their laughter echoed through the camp.

The draw to explore, however, proved too much for Sala to resist once Joram put the idea in her head. It had been impossible of late to sneak off pre-dawn, as she had been. But what if she had permission to search in the daylight? When her brother went off to report, Sala gave in to temptation and headed for the far side of the camp, where Mama helped catalog. With the outward semblance of patience, she waited for her mother to acknowledge her.

Her mother finished the entry she was working on before looking up. "Yes, Sala?"

With only a moment's hesitation, Sala ducked her head, then spoke, "Jory is back in camp. May I go exploring?"

Guilt fluttered in her belly. She had not lied with her words, but her mother would assume her brother would be accompanying her. She held still against the impulse to fidget as she waited.

Mama nodded. "Don't be long, though. You're to help prepare for dinner tonight."

"Yes'm," Sala called back, already heading for her treasured supplies, as eager to avoid any questions as she was to explore. She would return well before time to get ready for the evening meal. She had to be back before Akashi cut Joram loose...

With her pouch clutched in hand, she made her way past the wagons to the edge of camp. She glared as several of the other Roamer girls went by, tittering at her progress. Her steps grew increasingly awkward the more she hurried. Let them laugh; she couldn't afford to slow down. What she truly wanted was to run, but the skill was beyond her still-developing coordination. She finally reached the underbrush, glad of the gentle breeze to cool her. Probing through the flora, she discovered a small game trail, likely worn by djuri. Anyone else would have struggled through, but for once Sala was glad of her small stature. The path was perfect for her. Her gaze scoured the brush surrounding the trail, noting the familiar before swiftly moving on. Occasionally, she saw an unusual variant on a specimen she had catalogued before, but she wasn't here to find mutations or subphyla. Nothing short of a new discovery would satisfy her. Something of value. Something of sufficient note to outweigh her transgression, at the very least...

Sala didn't venture far at first. The sounds of camp remained a steady murmur in the background. Briefly, she stopped to sketch an unusual track, but with no other sign of what may have made it she moved on. Soon she got caught up in the hunt for *her* discovery, peering under rocks and bushes, stirring up the dirt. At one point she tried to climb up the trunk of an umbrella tree in pursuit of an insect she was certain she had never seen, even as a specimen or sketch, only to slide down and bark her shin, left ground-bound to watch as the insect disappeared into the foliage. And still she persisted until the murmur of the camp became a whisper. And then a memory, all but forgotten.

The fading light betrayed her, bringing Sala back from the tight focus of her hunt. As she finally noticed the onset of twilight her belly turned, fear and hunger warring in her gut. Distant birdsong filled her ears, nothing more. Whatever trail she'd followed had petered out. Her legs ached and every patch of bare skin bore at least one itching bite or burning scratch. She shivered and clutched the strap of her pouch. She turned in a slow, stumbling circle trying to see some sign of a path, or at the very least a break in the foliage showing the way she had come. But the gentle breeze had grown more forceful erasing any sign of her passage.

Sala could not silence her first whimper, but she ruthlessly strangled the rest. Though she desperately wanted to call out she knew she must not. Pawcats and demon dogs were drawn by sounds of distress. So were other predators. Maybe ones they didn't even know about yet. That she wouldn't know how to defend herself from. Becoming something's dinner was *not* how she wanted to make her new discovery.

Drawing a deep breath, she straightened her spine and calmed herself. If she hadn't been missed already, she would be soon. Someone would come looking for her. Yes, she had been foolish, but Joram had taught her how to survive as no one else had thought to. He believed in her. She would not disappoint him. The two things he taught her as most important were defense and shelter. *If we get separated arm yourself, then find a place you will be safe and stay there,* he'd said every time they'd gone exploring. *Let me come to you. I* will *find you.*

With the memory of his words firmly in her thoughts, she returned to searching the ground, this time for a long, stout branch, something she could use for both support and defense. As she searched she also looked for any source of shelter... an outcrop of rocks, the high roots of a glúin tree, a cave or overhang, anything she could put her back against. The best she could find was a stout twintree. If not for her small size it would have provided no shelter at all. If she could have climbed the tree, she would have, but that remained beyond her skill. As the sky grew darker, she huddled at the base of the trunks, her back pressed against the smooth bark.

In her pouch she had several nutrition bars and water still half-filled her flask, but fear gripped her tight at both belly and throat. The thought of eating or drinking made her feel sick. While the light remained, she watched the surrounding wilderness for movement, her ears straining for any sound that might be danger or deliverance. *Please, Joram,* Sala thought, *please find me soon.*

She struggled not to cry. 

Sala woke to a pair of glowing eyes staring out of the darkness.

She shrieked and fumbled for her stick. The eyes crouched lower, as if to pounce. They were joined by a second set. A low, barely heard rumbling came to her ears. By the height and the sound, Sala knew two juvenile pawcats stalked her. The twintree trunks pressed hard against her back as she tried to push herself to her feet. Her long trek and the chill from the ground had tightened her muscles, though, and she ended up tumbling back down. The glowing eyes leapt.

"Joram!" she cried out.

Seemingly out of nowhere—but more likely from the brush behind her—someone snatched Sala's branch from her hands. It wasn't her brother. In the dark, Sala could not make out who it was, but she would have known Joram in utter darkness, let alone starlight. This person stood shorter, slighter, but not by much. Sala's gaze followed the swing of the branch. With precision and force it connected with the leaping predator. She heard a thud, followed by the muffled crack of breaking bones. The creature's cry cut short, followed by brief thrashing that faltered, then stopped all together. Sala's savior raised the branch again, but the shadowy hulk of the second predator already skulked away, its grumbling whine fading with the growing distance.

The predators dealt with, the stranger turned. Something in those movements reminded Sala very much of the pawcat before it lay broken on the ground. The motions were fluid and powerful, dangerous and completely unfamiliar. Swallowing a whimper, Sala shrank back against the tree, her arms hugged around herself more for comfort than any sort of protection.

The form before her went still, then slowly crouched down where it stood, lowering to the ground until its legs were crossed and its hands laid down where a person's knees would be.

"It's okay, little one." The voice belonged to a woman. The words did nothing to reassure. Sala knew all the Roamers, from both bands; the woman was not one of them. She could have been from Artistos, but none of *them* would venture past their barrier, let along this far into Fremont's wilds.

The woman could only be one of the *altereds*.

Sala shrank more into herself, pressed harder into the tree, remembering the recent murmurings about camp. Silently, she begged Joram... or *someone* she knew to hurry.

There was a *click* and a soft, warm glow lit the woman's face.

Drawing a sharp breath, Sala straightened.

If anyone had asked her if she'd memories of the *altered* who fixed her, Sala would have said no, with full confidence. Until this moment, that would have been true, but those eyes... those electric green eyes staring back at her... Startling, but kind. Reassuring, and not for the first time. Sala found it did not matter to her that they were not natural in color.

"Why do you follow us?"

The eyes slowly blinked. The woman remained silent, her expression considering, the way Akashi looked when he carefully chose what words to say.

"To make sure you are well," the *altered* answered in a soft, calm tone. "To make sure what we have done still functions properly for you."

"How do you follow me?" Sala asked, now certain her earlier worry was founded.

The woman blinked again, only faster, as if Sala had startled her, then her eyes lowered slightly. "I am a wind reader... one engineered to read the data streams. The tech in your blood, that which repaired you, it speaks to me."

Sala thought on that, not certain how she felt about their 'tech' still being inside her. Surely Papa did not know. He would have been angry. Much more than angry. She prayed he never found out. She couldn't bear if his look toward her changed any more.

"Does that..." Sala's voice broke. "Does that make me... *altered*?"

Compassion softened the woman's eyes, but hurt shadowed them. "No, little one. No. Still your worries. We only repaired you, like setting a broken bone, or removing a tumor. We did not change you as we have been changed."

Sala did not know what to say. Or to believe. There was so much she didn't understand. And so many questions she wanted to ask... Before she could decide on the next, distant cries drew her attention away from the woman, her brother's voice among them.

Joram! He came, as he promised!

Even as joy and relief bubbled up from her heart, Sala's muscles knotted with worry. Not for herself, but for her rescuer. She was startled to discover she no longer feared the *altered* sitting before her. While Sala did not know the woman's name, she remembered her. Knew at some point the woman had comforted her and cared for her when they had remade her body. When she ventured out this day, she had not realized her new discovery would be a rediscovery. A faint recollection surfaced from the time of her surgery, something the woman had once said, which Sala's heart had held to fiercely, if not her memory. *Different is just different, not wrong.* Words that applied as much to Sala herself as to the *altered.*

Again, Sala heard her name called out, distracting her.

Her expression now wary, the woman rose with an ease Sala envied. Without another word, the *altered* stooped and picked up the carcass she had made.

"Wait," Sala called to her, almost whispering, though clearly the searchers were not close enough to hear her. The woman paused, turning to meet her gaze.

"Why... why did you come here?"

"To live free... without conflict."

Sala was old enough to recognize the wry twist to the woman's lips, but not old enough yet to know how to respond.

The woman gave Sala a sad smile, then she turned and left, parting the brush as if it were tissue, the pawcat casually draped over her shoulder. Her departure left no sign and made no sound as Joram's cries drew closer.

It was as if the woman had never been there. It was as if she never would be again.

In seemingly an instant, Sala grew up, and with sadness, she murmured, "I'm sorry."

For whatever little difference it made, in her heart, Sala knew the woman heard her.

About the Author

Award-winning author, editor, and publisher Danielle Ackley-McPhail has worked both sides of the publishing industry for longer than she cares to admit. In 2014 she joined forces with husband Mike McPhail and friend Greg Schauer to form her own publishing house, eSpec Books.

Her published works include seven novels, *Yesterday's Dreams, Tomorrow's Memories, Today's Promise, The Halfling's Court, The Redcaps' Queen, Daire's Devils,* and *Baba Ali and the Clockwork Djinn,* written with Day Al-Mohamed. She is also the author of the solo collections *Eternal Wanderings, A Legacy of Stars, Consigned to the Sea, Flash in the Can, Transcendence, Between Darkness and Light, The Fox's Fire, The Kindly One,* and the non-fiction writers' guides *The Literary Handyman, More Tips from the Handyman,* and *LH: Build-A-Book Workshop.* She is the senior editor of the *Bad-Ass Faeries* anthology series, *Gaslight & Grimm, Side of Good/Side of Evil, After Punk,* and *Footprints in the Stars.* Her short stories are included in numerous other anthologies and collections.

In addition to her literary acclaim, she crafts and sells original costume horns under the moniker The Hornie Lady Custom Costume Horns, and homemade flavor-infused candied ginger under the brand of Ginger KICK! at literary conventions, on commission, and wholesale.

Danielle lives in New Jersey with husband and fellow writer, Mike McPhail and four extremely spoiled cats.

Our CyberSupport

COSTRUENDO IL FRATELLINO

STEVEN RADECKI

TRADUZIONE DI FLAVIA IDÀ

Copertine realizzate da Niki Lenhart
nikilen-designs.com

Pubblicato da Paper Angel Press
paperangelpress.com

ISBN 978-1-953469-21-2 (Edizione tascabile)

10 9 8 7 6 5 4 3 2 1

PRIMA EDIZIONE

Per il mio Josh,
e all'uomo dalle grandi qualità che è diventato

1

"**P**APÀ, POSSO AVERE UN FRATELLINO?"
Mi fermai, con il mattoncino Lego in mano.

"Sei sicuro di volerlo?" risposi, cercando di apparire disinvolto. "Sai che dovresti aiutare a prenderti cura di lui. E si porterebbe via i tuoi giocattoli …"

"Lo so, papà".

Josh mi guardò esasperato. Non era la prima volta che toccavamo l'argomento. Non che io volessi privare Josh dell'esperienza. L'avevo fatta io stesso. Ma sapevo anche che avere un fratello non era solo fratellanza.

"D'accordo, Josh" dissi, posando il mattoncino. "Lascerò a te la scelta: un fratellino o troppi giocattoli".

Ammetto che era un po' un colpo basso. Ma era molto più facile che spiegargli la vera ragione.

Prima di rispondere, Josh diede una rapida occhiata alla sua stanza. Osservò la sua collezione di Lego e action figures, le sue pile di videogiochi.

"Troppi giocattoli" annunciò poi, facendo fermamente cenno di sì. Presa la decisione, tornò al progetto di costruzione che avevamo appena intrapreso, collocando un altro mattoncino Lego al suo posto.

L'ho scampata bella anche stavolta, pensai.

Quella sera, dopo aver finalmente messo a letto Josh, mi sedetti alla scrivania con l'intenzione di pagare le bollette e di occuparmi di altre faccende di contabilità domestica. Notai che s'era fatto molto più tardi di quanto credessi. Pensai di rimandare ancora una volta tutte quelle seccanti incombenze, ma già sapevo che la sera seguente non sarebbe stata più proficua di questa. È incredibile a quante scuse e tattiche di procrastinazione ricorrono i bambini, invece di semplicemente chiudere gli occhi e andare a dormire. Probabilmente però non meno sorprendente di quando ti distrai per un istante, poi ti giri e li vedi respirare tranquillamente sul cuscino.

Tanto vale che finisco di farle, queste seccanti incombenze, mi spronai, sopprimendo a stento uno sbadiglio. *La maggior parte di questa gente generalmente parlando esige che le bollette siano pagate in tempo.*

Sarà forse curioso, ma preferisco lavorare in silenzio. Di notte, però, quando sono assorto in questo genere di compiti di routine, trovo piacevole un po' di musica di sottofondo — qualcosa a basso volume che mi permetta di sentire Josh se ha bisogno di me.

Non avevo molta voglia di musica, sicché accesi il piccolo televisore che tenevo su un armadietto a lato della scrivania. Lo schermo s'aprì sulla sanguinosa scena di una serie poliziesca.

Se voglio vedere questa robaccia guardo il telegiornale ...

Cambiai canale. Poi ancora. E poi ancora.

Ben presto persi la speranza di trovare qualcosa che non fosse o un brutale programma per adulti o un conduttore di talk show che chiacchierava sulle ultime novità geopolitiche con scintillanti celebrità venute più che altro a discutere i loro nuovi film, serie televisive, tour di concerti, intervallo di riabilitazione o combinazioni varie di tutto il suddetto.

Le mie dita si fermarono sul telecomando quando vidi un bambino dagli occhi da cerbiatto che scivolava attraverso una penombra azzurra sullo sfondo di una collina illuminata dalla luna. Lo riconobbi subito da una scena dell'ultimo film di fantascienza di Kubrick. Non era il film di Kubrick che preferivo; non era neanche uno dei peggiori, ma in ogni caso non avevo intenzione di guardarlo.

Forse era desiderio di evasione, forse semplicemente stanchezza, ma continuavo a distrarmi dalle bollette alle quali avrei dovuto prestare attenzione. Osservavo il bambino artificiale sullo schermo del televisore, e ad un tratto presi a chiedermi se fosse davvero possibile crearne uno.

Il software probabilmente avrei potuto idearlo. Di professione progetto e sviluppo programmi per computer. Cerco di far fare ai miei programmi ciò che i miei clienti desiderano fare, di produrre i risultati che essi desiderano. In genere non progetto o monto i veri e propri circuiti o componenti; quello lo lascio fare agli ingegneri elettrici e meccanici. Ero certo che non sarei mai stato in grado di mettere assieme un essere cibernetico complesso come quello del film.

Quando finalmente andai a letto, mi accorsi che non riuscivo a distogliere la mente dall'idea. Provai a dirmi che c'erano realtà tecnologiche e finanziarie da prendere in considerazione, realtà serie abbastanza da rendere il progetto quasi impossibile da portare a termine senza l'aiuto di nessuno.

Incapace di mettere a tacere il richiamo che continuava ad occupare i miei pensieri, alla fine decisi che semplicemente pensarci mi costava poco — a parte forse la perdita di qualche ora di sonno oppure qualche sogno inconsueto. Sicché chiusi gli occhi e mi lasciai andare alle fantasticherie.

Cominciavo a rendermi conto che l'idea era non solo possibile ma forse anche realizzabile con componenti facilmente reperibili nei negozi di elettronici. Se non fossi riuscito a trovare in un negozio ciò che mi occorreva, conoscevo molti amici che lavoravano presso alcune delle principali compagnie di computer e che forse sarebbero stati in grado di fornirmi quanto mi serviva. Mi misi perfino a fare un'ipotetica lista della spesa: scheda madre, chip di memoria, dischi rigidi …

Pur senza illudermi che sarei riuscito a creare qualcosa di sofisticato come il bambino artificiale del film di Kubrick — né creature artificiali di *qualunque* altro film — nell'arco di una sera ero passato da "È impossibile!" a "Cosa ci sarebbe di tanto difficile?"

Si da' il caso che fu più difficile di quanto credessi. Molto più difficile.

2

V I RISPARMIO I DETTAGLI DI COME LO FECI. Non solo perché devo tenere sottochiave la maggior parte dei dettagli finché non verrà risolta la questione del brevetto, ma anche perché probabilmente i dettagli interesserebbero unicamente ad altri esperti di computer o ad ingegneri elettrici. Alcuni di loro senza dubbio indicherebbero subito ognuno dei miei errori e ognuno dei modi in cui avrei potuto evitarli. Il punto comunque è: *l'ho fatto*.

Molte settimane dopo, aspettai impaziente che Josh tornasse a casa. Sua madre se l'era preso per il fine settimana, ma ci eravamo accordati che lo avrebbe riportato un giorno prima del solito, dato che la mattina seguente lei sarebbe partita per un viaggio d'affari. Io non mi ero lamentato; penso che anche Josh non avesse obiezioni.

Sarebbero arrivati nel tardo pomeriggio, circa un'ora prima di cena, ed era appena passato mezzogiorno. Sicché andavo nervosamente su e giù per la stanza, continuando a guardare l'orologio. Poi, non vedendoli arrivare all'ora promessa, cominciai a borbottare imprecazioni varie. Dopo quasi trenta minuti — benché mi parvero molti di più — sentii l'auto che parcheggiava. Aprii subito la porta d'ingresso mentre Carolyn e Josh erano ancora a qualche passo di distanza. Carolyn si fermò, spalancando gli occhi quando mi vide. Il suo volto era tutto un'espressione di critica.

Non mi ero guardato allo specchio, ma avevo un'immagine mentale abbastanza chiara di come doveva presentarsi il mio aspetto. Nei giorni trascorsi avevo dormito pochissimo, trascinandomi quasi sull'orlo dell'esaurimento, e la mia unica fonte di nutrizione erano stati cibi precotti da preparare velocemente nel microonde o da consumare direttamente dalla confezione. Non toccavo un rasoio da minimo tre giorni, e certamente dovevo avere gli occhi pesti per la mancanza di sonno. Se non altro comunque ero sicuro di non essere così maleodorante come sembravo. Mi ero fatto la doccia — benché avessi concesso a malincuore quei minuti necessari all'igiene personale e alla cortesia verso gli altri, mentre mi affannavo a finire il progetto prima che Josh arrivasse.

In un certo senso tutto ciò mi ricordava le notti insonni prima degli esami universitari. Ma era una rassomiglianza più che altro nostalgica; a quell'epoca ero stato molto più giovane. Sapevo che ora invece ne avrei probabilmente risentito per vari giorni a venire. Una cosa avevo imparato con gli anni: mai sottovalutare l'importanza di una buona dormita.

Josh mi guardò incuriosito, osservandomi più a lungo del solito. Non fece commenti mentre mi passava davanti, tirandosi dietro la sua valigetta. In genere non parlava molto durante le prime ore dopo che tornava da me. Quel giorno non si annunciava diverso dagli altri. Ma ciò non mi dava fastidio, sapendo quale fantastica sorpresa gli tenevo da parte nel seminterrato.

Carolyn apettava sui gradini della porta d'ingresso con l'aria di volersi spicciare. Questa era la parte sgradevole. Ero ansioso di mostrare il risultato della mia opera a Josh, ma non a Carolyn

— almeno non subito; al tempo stesso non potevo semplicemente mandarla via. Sicché tirai un lungo sospiro, che non credo le nascose il mio stato d'animo.

"Ti va di entrare per un paio di minuti?" le chiesi.

"Certo" mi rispose brusca, gettandomi un'altra occhiata di disapprovazione mentre entrava. Ero certo che si stava chiedendo se la casa fosse nelle stesse condizioni in cui ero io.

Fui sorpreso che lei avesse acconsentito ad entrare. Soffermarsi da me era una cosa che in genere preferiva non fare. Mi resi conto che ciò significava che aveva qualcosa da dirmi, e le nostre conversazioni erano raramente piacevoli.

La prima cosa che fece fu darmi una grossa busta. I muscoli del mio collo e delle mie spalle si fecero nodi d'acciaio. Erano mesi che cercavamo di finalizzare i termini del divorzio. Presupposi automaticamente che la busta contenesse un ennesimo fascio di astrusi documenti legali che sarei stato costretto a decifrare nella speranza che si potesse finalmente arrivare a un accordo tollerabile per entrambi.

"Josh ha una gita scolastica la settimana prossima" disse. "Questi sono i permessi firmati".

Presi la busta senza darci un'occhiata. I miei muscoli si rilassarono un poco.

"Ho anche ordinato dei biscotti alla pasticceria" aggiunse Carolyn. Lo disse a bassa voce e distogliendo gli occhi, come ammettendo che fare un gesto altruista per la scuola di Josh le dava un male fisico.

Accennando vagamente di sì, presi un appunto mentale di fare anch'io un gesto altruista per la scuola di Josh. Mi ricordai che quando lo avevo portato a scuola venerdì mattina, Josh mi aveva parlato di una raccolta fondi di qualche genere.

Carolyn si allontanò da me senza guardarmi. Un attimo dopo sentii la porta del bagno che si chiudeva.

Osservai la busta che tenevo in mano, cercando di decidere dove conservarla cosicché potessi ricordarmi di darla a Josh la mattina di lunedì, prima che andasse a scuola. Mentre ero intento a decidere, Josh tornò e mi diede un abbraccio veloce ma sincero.

"Ciao, papà".

Gli sorrisi, poi mi chinai verso di lui perché potessimo guardarci faccia a faccia. Tutto a un tratto notai che non dovevo chinarmi tanto in basso come prima.

"Ehilà, giovanotto. Ti sei divertito?"

Josh fece una scrollata di spalle.

Quel semplice gesto rivelava molto. Per quanto lo riguardava, qualunque cosa lui e sua madre avessero fatto assieme lo aveva interessato ben poco. Carolyn, probabilmente occupata con le preparazioni per il suo viaggio d'affari, doveva averlo semplicemente trascinato da un'incombenza all'altra. Volevo sentirmi irritato, ma ero troppo stanco e troppo ansioso per trovare l'indignazione necessaria.

"Ascolta" dissi sottovoce, sorridendo di nuovo ma non esageratamente, per non insospettirlo, il che non mi fu facile. "Ho da farti vedere una cosa —"

"È un segreto? O sono invitate anche le ragazze?"

Continuavo a guardare Josh, ma le guance mi si erano quasi arrossite. Non avevo sentito Carolyn tornare dal bagno. Sorpreso, dovetti fare uno sforzo per non cadere in avanti. Non si trattava esattamente che volessi tenerle nascosto il mio progetto. Si trattava solo che non avevo previsto la sua presenza quando lo avrei svelato a Josh.

"Pensi che sia un segreto?" chiesi a Josh.

Josh scrollò di nuovo le spalle. "D'accordo, immagino di sì" disse.

Con la coda dell'occhio notai che, a giudicare dalla sua espressione, Carolyn non era molto contenta dello scarso entusiasmo di Josh. Ma lasciai perdere. Era problema di Carolyn, non mio, e non lo avrei fatto ricadere su nostro figlio, non in quel momento.

"Allora va bene" risposi, facendo del mio meglio per sembrare sinceramente entusiasta, ma incapace di guardare Carolyn negli occhi. "Venite con me".

Mi alzai e porsi la mano a Josh. Lui l'afferrò saldamente, e tutti e tre ci avviammo verso il seminterrato.

Avevo attenuato le luci, più che altro per effetto drammatico. Se Carolyn e Josh avessero cercato di sbirciare nella semioscurità, non sarebbero riusciti a vedere granché.

Coperto da un telo scuro e illuminato solo da scarsa luce riflessa, ciò che giaceva sul mio banco da lavoro appariva come nient'altro che un oggetto informe dalle grandi dimensioni.

Carolyn e Josh si avvicinarono ad esso, muovendosi cautamente nella penombra. Alzai la mano per fermarli prima che lo toccassero.

"Un attimo".

Accesi la luce e mi chinai di nuovo verso Josh.

"Josh? Ricordi quante volte mi hai chiesto un fratellino?" Sorrisi. Josh mi seguì con lo sguardo mentre mi avvicinavo al banco da lavoro. Con un gesto probabilmente troppo grandioso, sollevai il telo.

"Ti presento il Fratellino 1.0!"

Dapprima Josh lo guardò fisso, senza comprendere. Un istante dopo spalancò gli occhi. Devo ammettere che si spalancò anche il mio amor proprio.

"Papà!" gridò "è fantastico!"

Fece un lento giro del banco da lavoro, studiando ogni particolare della mia creatura, senza avvicinarsi troppo. Mi accorsi che, nonostante la sua accesa curiosità, rimaneva un po' incerto. I miei occhi seguirono i suoi mentre osservava la figura immobile davanti a noi.

Avevo abbigliato il fratellino di vestiti che a Josh non entravano più. Non entravano molto bene neanche alla mia creatura, ma senz'altro aiutavano a farla sembrare più reale, benché a guardarla da vicino si sarebbe notato subito che non lo era. Mi chiesi preoccupato se abbigliarla avrebbe dato adito a imbarazzanti domande sulla sua correttezza anatomica. Se la domanda fosse sorta, la risposta sarebbe stata "No". Non c'era affatto bisogno che questa particolare creatura fosse "perfettamente funzionante".

I capelli erano artificiali, creati utilizzando una parrucca di poco prezzo acquistata in un negozio di costumi. Mi auguravo che sembrassero veri abbastanza da far chiedere a chi li guardava se erano veri o no. Avevo pensato anche ad aggiungere sopracciglia e ciglia. Per queste ultime avevo impiegato parecchie più ore di quanto avessi immaginato. Da ciò credo di avere tratto una maggiore comprensione del motivo per cui alcune donne ci mettono tanto per truccarsi.

Le mani però … le mani erano uno dei miei tocchi più ispirati. Dapprima avevo pensato di nasconderne i meccanismi interni con spessi guanti di latex, ripromettendomi di trovare più in là qualcosa di maggiormente realistico. Un giorno, però, mentre stavo facendo compere — non ricordo cosa cercassi — mi capitò di vedere in un negozio uno scatolone di costumi di Halloween a prezzi ridotti.

Là, in mezzo a un mucchio di articoli fatti teoricamente per incutere paura, disgusto o tutt'e due le cose, notai un avambraccio mozzato fatto di gomma. Passata la mia revulsione iniziale, mi resi conto di aver trovato la soluzione. Ispezionandolo da vicino, e senza dubbio attirando sguardi di curiosità e disapprovazione dagli altri clienti del negozio, mi accorsi che era molto simile a uno spesso guanto. Flessibile e cavo, mi avrebbe permesso di celare parte della struttura del braccio, e sarebbe stato molto più verosimile di tutto ciò che avevo cercato di escogitare prima.

La vera difficoltà si rivelò trovare una mano destra e una sinistra che corrispondessero. Rovistai nello scatolone per vari minuti. Immagino fosse una scena alquanto macabra; un signore dall'apparenza perbene che rovistava eccitato in un cumulo di arti mozzati. Conoscete la frase: *Sono sempre i tipi riservati e rispettabili ...*

Scoprii subito che c'era, come del resto c'è in tutto il mondo, una preponderanza di mani destre. Stavo per abbandonare la mia ricerca quando vidi non una ma due mani sinistre quasi nascoste in fondo al mucchio. Le presi subito entrambe; meglio averne una di ricambio, pensai.

Si adattavano perfettamente allo scopo. Entravano un po' strette, ma ragionai che tanto avrei dovuto toglierle e rimetterle solo poche volte. Tagliai via gli orli irregolari e dipinti di rosso, per farle sembrare meno macabre. Da vicino si vedeva che ovviamente non erano rivestite di pelle umana, ma solo se uno le guardava una seconda volta.

Josh rimase in silenzio, osservandomi con gli occhi pieni di meraviglia.

"Può parlare? Cosa può fare? Può camminare?" chiese senza fiato.

"Non ancora" risposi. "Ma forse un giorno ... chissà".

Josh sembrò deluso.

"Voglio dire" mi corressi subito "non può ancora camminare. Ma *può* parlare ... e può aiutarti a fare molte cose. Ha imparato molto, ed è capace di imparare ancora di più. E le braccia funzionano ... più o meno".

Josh sembrava perplesso.

"Le mani non sono molto precise" ammisi. "Sono in grado di raccogliere quasi tutto tranne oggetti molto piccoli. Oggetti più piccoli di ... diciamo un mattoncino Lego, con quelli avrebbe difficoltà".

Di quest'ultima cosa confesso che ero alquanto compiaciuto. Non era stato complicato far sì che ognuna delle dita si muovesse indipendentemente dalle altre, ma non avevo avuto tempo di calibrarle perché potessero muoversi in combinazione. Erano in grado di indicare una certa direzione, ma non proprio di fare il saluto vulcaniano.

Josh sembrò soddisfatto della mia risposta. Allungò cauto la mano e sfiorò la creatura con un dito. A quella distanza si vedeva subito che il fratellino era ricoperto di latex. Mi ripromettevo di apportare miglioramenti più in là, a quello e a tante altre cose.

"Come si accende?" chiese Josh, movendo la testa alla ricerca dell'interruttore.

"Oh … Devi semplicemente dargli un comando verbale. È programmato per rispondere alla tua voce."

Josh osservò da vicino il volto della creatura.

"Davvero?"

Feci cenno di sì, sorridendo. Lui esitava incerto.

"Su, prova" gli dissi.

Guardò me, poi la creatura ancora inerte sul banco di lavoro. Infine esclamò: "Svegliati!"

Il comando era più forte del necessario, ma non dissi nulla anzi risi fra me, compiaciuto del suo entusiasmo.

Dapprima non accadde nulla. Gli occhi di tutti e tre noi rimanevano fissi sull'oggetto immobile mentre aspettavamo ansiosi, trattenendo il respiro. Josh non sorrideva più, anzi mi guardava deluso con i suoi occhi di un azzurro glaciale. Cominciai ad agitarmi preoccupato.

"*Diamine*" pensai "*Proprio adesso?*"

Andai a controllare i monitor dei meccanismi interni. Da quanto si poteva vedere, ogni cosa era a posto. Alle mie spalle sentii il sommesso, quasi impercettibile suono della creatura che si risvegliava. Tirai un sospiro di sollievo, tornando accanto al banco da lavoro.

Le palpebre della creatura si sollevarono e si abbassarono. Poi nient'altro. Ricominciai a preoccuparmi. Un istante dopo gli occhi cominciarono ad aprirsi e a chiudersi in rapida successione e a intervalli casuali, esattamente secondo il mio programma.

"Ehilà" disse Josh a voce inconsuetamente alta, facendomi pensare che stesse per mettersi a ridacchiare. Quasi in un sussurro aggiunse "… fratellino".

Lo sguardo della creatura si rivolse verso di lui.

"Salve, Josh".

Gli occhi di Josh si fecero ancora più stupiti. La creatura parlava con voce di bambino; un po' piatta, ma riconoscibile come voce di bambino.

Mi ci era voluto molto tempo per perfezionare la voce. Nella mia mente l'avevo ideata con precisione, facendo il processo inverso a quello che generalmente si fa, cioè immaginare come suona la voce di una persona basandosi sull'aspetto di essa. In questo caso, avevo appunto immaginato la voce della mia creatura basandomi sull'aspetto che le avevo dato. Non era stato affatto facile trovare prima il codice giusto e poi modificarlo perché corrispondesse alla mia ideazione. Ci avevo quasi rinunciato più di una volta, ma ogni volta avevo deciso di procedere, finché c'ero riuscito.

"Può mettersi a sedere?" chiese Josh.

"Certo!" risposi sorridendo. "Ma dovremo aiutarlo".

Feci scivolare la mano sotto la spalla sinistra del fratellino. "Ecco. Dammi una mano".

Con molta più cautela di quanto fosse necessario, Josh mise la mano sotto la spalla destra e mi aiutò come meglio poté a sollevarlo in posizione seduta con le gambe penzolanti dal bordo del banco da lavoro. Udii il suono rassicurante di ingranaggi che scattavano obbedienti. La creatura ora rassomigliava in modo sorprendente a un vero bambino seduto sul lettino da visita di un dottore. Quasi mi aspettavo che saltasse giù e corresse via.

Josh mi tornò accanto. La testa meccanica della creatura seguì il movimento. Josh studiò ancora una volta il suo nuovo compagno di giochi.

"Posso portarlo in camera mia?"

"Certo" risposi un po' sorpreso. "Non vedo perché no".

Josh fece per muoversi, poi si fermò, facendo un vago gesto indicante che non sapeva come farlo.

"Lo porto su io" dissi, accennando alle scale. "Intanto va' a vedere se in camera tua la sediolina è vuota".

Dubitavo che lo fosse. La sediolina a dondolo era il luogo preferito dove Josh ammucchiava praticamente tutto ciò che gli chiedevo di non lasciare ammucchiato sul pavimento. Josh era capace di fare le cose diabolicamente alla lettera se gli faceva comodo.

"Ti aiuto" disse Carolyn, seguendo Josh su per la scala. Ma Josh se la lasciò dietro in un baleno, scomparendo alla vista prima che il piede di lei si posasse sul terzo scalino.

Carolyn si fermò dov'era e mi guardò a lungo fissamente. Non penso che approvasse il mio progetto. Mi chiesi cosa la infastidisse di più: che non le avessi detto nulla o che un uomo adulto avesse dedicato tutto quel tempo e tutta quell'energia alla costruzione di un aggeggio del genere. Mi chiesi anche se valesse la pena di curarsi della sua opinione. Poi, sospirando fra me, riportai la mia attenzione al banco da lavoro.

Sollevai la creatura prendendola con attenzione per le ginocchia e le spalle. Era molto più leggera di quanto mi fosse sembrata prima; direi che pesava più o meno quanto Josh. Presi nel loro insieme, i suoi componenti elettronici non erano più pesanti di ossa, pelle e muscoli umani. Erano quasi tutti fatti di metallo e di gomma, eppure ciò faceva sembrare la creatura ancora più delicata e fragile. Me l'appoggiai con cura sul petto. Molto probabilmente si sarebbe creduto che stessi trasportando un vero bambino.

Salii le scale con goffa lentezza, timoroso di inciampare da un momento all'altro. Se fossi caduto, non mi facevo illusioni su chi di noi due avrebbe subito danni maggiori.

Arrivato sul ballatoio emisi un sospiro di sollievo, poi portai la creatura nella camera di Josh. Notai con sorpresa che un'ampia area del pavimento era sgombra; sbirciai sotto il letto, poi verso la porta dell'armadio.

*Meglio non avvicinarsi all'armadio … * mi dissi. Senza dubbio Josh aveva stipato tutto là dentro.

Con molta cura poggiai la mia creatura sulla sediolina a dondolo. Vi rimase in una posizione rigida, limitata dalla sua anatomia metallica. Non che la posizione gli causasse danno, ma era decisamente antiestetica.

Il mio sguardo si fermò su un cuscino lasciato sul pavimento. Lo presi e lo feci scivolare con attenzione dietro la schiena della creatura; la quale adesso era piegata in avanti, come se scrutando con intenso interesse ciò che la circondava. Quel piccolo ma discernibile miglioramento mise a tacere le mie remore di esteta.

Josh non mi prestava alcuna attenzione, tutto preso a rovistare in un contenitore di plastica di medie dimensioni. Trovato quanto cercava, si accosciò accanto alla creatura curva in avanti nella sediolina a dondolo.

"Questi sono i Lego" le disse, aprendo le mani come a svelare un tesoro; e i Lego, come ogni genitore sa, sono un tesoro.

Ne scelse due e li mise assieme. "Si aggiungono così" spiegò. "Vedi?"

Con un lieve fruscìo meccanico, il braccio del fratellino si sollevò. Josh gli mise in mano i due Lego. La mano s'alzò e il fratellino li studiò attentamente.

"Lego" disse dopo un attimo, indicando che comprendeva.

Josh fece un enorme sorriso. "Sì!"

Portò un tavolino di plastica davanti al fratellino; raccolse una grossa manciata di Lego e ve l'ammucchiò sopra.

"Ecco" disse soddisfatto. Guardò me e Carolyn. "Tu e mamma potete andarvene" aggiunse, rinchiudendosi nel suo mondo. La sua attenzione ora era interamente concentrata sul suo nuovo compagno di giochi. Non aveva più bisogno del nostro intervento.

Scossi lievemente la testa, sorridendo fra me, compiaciuto che Josh avesse accolto il fratellino subito. Mi ero preoccupato di ciò; di solito Josh non faceva amicizia facilmente.

Mentre uscivo notai l'espressione di Carolyn. Era palese che, al contrario di me, non era entusiasta. Per un attimo pensai che sarebbe testardamente rimasta indietro. Ma quando si rese conto che Josh non aveva più intenzione di badare a nessuno di noi due, mi seguì fuori.

"Devo andare" disse nel salotto, con un tono di voce che non mi piacque. "Torno fra due settimane", aggiunse, raccogliendo la borsa dal tavolo. "Quel weekend Josh lo prendo io".

Feci cenno di sì. Anche se avessi voluto dire qualcosa, non avrei saputo cosa. Carolyn aveva semplicemente reiterato i termini del nostro accordo di custodia.

"Buon viaggio" dissi sincero.

"Grazie" rispose, in un tono che mi riportò alla mente il perché ci eravamo separati.

Rimasi sulla porta finché l'auto non si allontanò, poi rivolsi la mia attenzione a cosa preparare per cena.

3

L A MATTINA SEGUENTE, QUANDO JOSH ENTRÒ IN CUCINA, fui sorpreso di vedere che si era alzato così presto, e ancora più sorpreso di vederlo già vestito invece che ancora in pigiama. Quasi ogni mattina dovevo sollevarlo di peso dal letto. Era una novità che oggi non mi avesse costretto a farlo uscire dalla sua stanza, ora che gli avevo permesso di tenersi il fratellino in camera sua. In ogni caso, gli spiegai che il fratellino non aveva bisogno di dormire.

"Perfetto" disse Josh con aria da esperto. "Così potrà vegliare su di me tutta la notte".

"Hmm, beh" risposi, cercando di trovare un buon argomento contrario. "A dire il vero non è programmato per quello". Mi preoccupava l'idea che Josh sarebbe rimasto tutta la notte a giocare con lui.

"Vuol dire che non può?" insisté Josh. "Però può sempre guardare fuori dalla finestra e controllare sotto il letto, no?"

"Hmm, beh" ripetei. "Immagino di sì." Il che non era vero.

Mi arresi. S'era già fatto tardi; se Josh si sentiva rassicurato credendosi sotto la protezione di un robot, perché contraddirlo. E poi, forse un giorno il robot sarebbe stato in grado di proteggerlo davvero.

Ecco una cosa da aggiungere, pensai, con la mente già al lavoro su come incorporare nella mia creazione un sistema d'allarme.

Abbracciai Josh. "Buongiorno, giovanotto".

Come sua madre, Josh non è mattiniero. Con lui è meglio cominciare piano, con frasi semplici.

"Cosa ti va per colazione?"

Non rispose subito, assorto. Poi fece un gran sorriso di assoluta certezza. "Gavin ed io stamattina vogliamo le frittelle con lo sciroppo ".

Spalancai un po' gli occhi.

Gavin?

Mi resi conto che era giusto dare un nome al nuovo membro della nostra famiglia. Ma perché proprio quel nome?

Stavo per chiederglielo, ma s'era fatto davvero tardi. Mi avviai verso la credenza. Non c'era tempo per preparare le frittelle da zero; poi mi ricordai che forse avevo una miscela pronta avanzata da una delle nostre gite in campeggio con i Cub Scout.

"D'accordo" dissi. "Ma senza gingillarsi".

"Perfetto" rispose allegro Josh. "Ora vado a prendere Gavin".

Feci segno di sì distrattamente, cercando di ricordare dove avevo messo quella miscela per frittelle che non riuscivo a trovare. Mi ci volle un attimo per cogliere quanto aveva detto Josh.

Una cascata di immagini si presentò alla mia mente: Josh che trascinava Gavin giù per le scale, con la testa del fratellino meccanico che sbatteva contro ogni scalino; Josh che cercava di portare giù Gavin allo stesso modo in cui io lo avevo portato su, poi ruzzolare a capofitto. Gavin *probabilmente* non avrebbe riportato grandi danni, ma Josh sicuramente sì. Mi precipitai verso le scale prima che mi saltasse in mente un'altra scena disastrosa.

Troppo tardi. Ero ancora nel salotto quando vidi una piccola mano che afferrava la ringhiera. Poi vidi una delle scarpe di Josh che si muoveva con estrema cautela. Sembrava una di quelle scene di film girate esageratamente al rallentatore che presagiscono qualcosa di terribile.

Un attimo dopo si vide l'altra scarpa che si posava sullo scalino di sotto. Poi apparve il torso di Josh, che teneva la mano saldamente sulla ringhiera e allentava la presa appena quanto bastava per continuare la discesa. Infine emerse la testa di mio figlio. Quasi scoppiai a ridere, sia per sollievo che in apprezzamento della sua destrezza.

Portava il fratellino sulle spalle a mo' di zaino, piegato sotto il peso come un gobbetto nano, con ciascuna delle braccia di Gavin appese a ciascuna spalla. Quasi mi affrettai ad aiutarlo, ma era chiaro che non aveva bisogno della mia assistenza. Lo osservai mentre scendeva, finché non fu arrivato all'ultimo scalino.

Josh sembrava sorpreso, come non rendendosi conto di avercela fatta, poi sorrise trionfante. Era stato così preso dal suo compito che non s'era accorto di me. Quando mi vide, aggrottò la fronte, aspettandosi che io lo rimproverassi. Invece rimasi in silenzio, mentre lui portava il fratellino in cucina.

4

JOSH TRASCORREVA MOLTO TEMPO con il suo compagno di giochi meccanico.

In maggior parte si dedicavano a ciò che amano i bambini di quell'età: fantasiose creazioni Lego, videogiochi e programmi televisivi. Ovviamente era perlopiù Josh che creava e giocava mentre Gavin lo stava a guardare; ma spesso Josh gli poneva domande.

Nella maggior parte dei casi, la risposta di Gavin era "Non so"; a volte era "Sì"; ma non era mai "No" — almeno non quando ero presente ad ascoltare.

Ecco una cosa curiosa, pensai, ricordando che "No!" è spesso la prima parola che un bambino impara, molto probabilmente perché è la parola che sente più spesso in sua presenza.

Josh non si lagnava mai dei limiti di Gavin. Aveva afferrato il concetto che non ero in grado di perfezionarlo in tutto. Trattava Gavin con ogni cura, come mi aveva promesso di fare se io gli avessi dato un fratellino di carne e ossa. Ovviamente con Gavin avevo il vantaggio di non dovergli mai cambiare il pannolino, né preoccuparmi che prendesse il raffreddore o facesse le bizze. Di quando in quando c'era qualche problema tecnico, ma nulla che non potessi correggere. Quasi senza che nessuno di noi se ne rendesse conto, Gavin e le sue poche necessità essenziali ben presto entrarono a far parte della nostra vita quotidiana.

Qualche settimana dopo, un pomeriggio dissi ai due bambini di andare a giocare fuori. Gavin non aveva bisogno di sole e aria aperta, ma Josh senz'altro sì. Riluttante ad allontanarsi dal suo videogioco favorito, Josh finalmente — e a malincuore — fu d'accordo che l'alleanza ribelle sarebbe *probabilmente* riuscita a fare a meno del suo aiuto per un paio d'ore, e lui e Gavin andarono a giocare in giardino.

Josh portò giù Gavin con praticata destrezza, poi lo depose nella sedia a rotelle di seconda mano che avevo acquistato per quello scopo. Insieme uscirono e andarono a sedersi nell'angolo del giardino dov'era lo scivolo di plastica che io e Carolyn avevamo comprato per lui. Compiaciuto di quel piccolo successo, cominciai a fare le faccende domestiche della giornata. I mesi estivi, quando Josh non era a scuola, erano sempre un po' più complicati. Durante l'anno scolastico potevo cambiare le lenzuola del suo letto o riordinare i suoi vestiti senza dovermi preoccupare di disturbarlo. Quando era in casa, era meno facile trovare ritagli di tempo ininterrotto.

Dopo un'ora o giù di lì, sentii Josh che mi chiamava.

"Papà!"

Dapprima pensai che stesse cercando di attirare la mia attenzione per farmi vedere qualche sua scoperta. Mi asciugai le mani e gettai un'occhiata dalla porta del giardino. Le scoperte di Josh erano solitamente animaletti morti: uccellini, lucertole, topolini, serpentelli. Josh era sempre affascinato dagli animaletti morti, io non tanto. Posai lo strofinaccio e mi avviai verso la porta.

Non dirmi che hai trovato un altro —

"PAPÀ!"

Mi misi a correre.

Josh era davanti allo scivolo, con gli occhi fissi al suolo, tremante. Gavin era steso a terra, con braccia e gambe piegate ad angoli che non potrebbero mai essere stati quelli di un essere umano nelle stesse condizioni. Provai un enorme sollievo quando aprì gli occhi.

Un vero bambino avrebbe gridato di dolore, mentre Gavin semplicemente rimaneva là steso. I comandi elettronici avevano probabilmente segnalato il danno, ma non avevo provveduto a installare un sistema che specificasse quale genere di danno. Sapevo di poterlo chiedere direttamente a Gavin, ma in quel momento non riuscivo a parlare. Una parte di me voleva aggrapparsi all'illusione che era un vero bambino, che dalla sua bocca non sarebbero uscite solo complicate formule tecniche. Sicché non dissi nulla.

Josh si fece di lato, gli occhi lucidi di lacrime trattenute a stento.

"Mi dispiace, papà" disse con voce strozzata. "Non l'ho fatto apposta, lo giuro. Non sapevo …"

Lo abbracciai forte, mentre lui scoppiava a piangere, atterrito e sconvolto. Gli accarezzai i capelli e cercai di calmarlo, di fargli capire che non ero arrabbiato.

Dopo un po' Josh smise di piangere, tirando su col naso. Lo lasciai andare; lui si allontanò da me, con gli occhi rossi e gonfi. Si asciugò le guance, poi indicò Gavin.

"Papà?" mi chiese con la voce che gli tremava. "Puoi aggiustarlo?"

Guardai Gavin steso sull'erba. Il danno non sembrava irrimediabile, ma non vedevo l'ora di andare a controllare.

Sorrisi a mio figlio. "Certo. Sono sicuro che lo rimetteremo assieme in un baleno".

Josh mi ricambiò il sorriso, con più fiducia in me di quanta io ne avessi in me stesso. Gli diedi un colpetto sulla spalla, poi rivolsi di nuovo la mia attenzione a Gavin.

A parte il braccio decisamente deformato, dall'esterno non notavo altri danni. Ma esitavo a toccarlo, memore delle mie lezioni di pronto soccorso; la prima cosa che insegnano è di non spostare la vittima, in caso la spina dorsale sia compromessa.

Quasi sorrisi. Gavin aveva infatti qualcosa di simile a una spina dorsale, un meccanismo il cui scopo era di mantenerlo dritto quando era in piedi o seduto. C'erano alcuni cavi attaccati ad esso, ma danneggiarli non voleva dire interferire con il suo funzionamento.

Lo sollevai con cura. Il suo braccio slogato pendeva, dondolando mentre lo portavo in casa. Josh mi seguì senza parlare, rimanendo un po' indietro. Anche Gavin non parlava; mi guardava fisso, con un'espressione stranamente vuota.

Scesi nel seminterrato e fui sollevato di vedere che sul banco da lavoro era stesa una coperta. Gavin si sarebbe trovato più comodo che sulla nuda superficie di metallo. Lo misi giù, lasciando che il braccio ferito penzolasse dal bordo del banco da lavoro. Per un istante mi chiesi se sarebbe bastato sforzare il braccio nella posizione corretta; poi abbandonai l'idea, non sapendo se in quel modo lo avrei danneggiato ancora di più.

Mi allontanai di qualche passo, per soppesare la situazione con maggiore obiettività. Probabilmente avrei dovuto staccare del tutto il braccio dalla spalla ... Guardai Josh. Non ero sicuro che Josh sarebbe stato in grado di essere presente all'operazione, benché sapesse che Gavin non era fatto di carne e ossa.

Non ci sarebbe stato sangue, pensai. *Solo cavi e circuiti elettronici. Però chissà ...*

Infine decisi di lasciare la scelta a Josh. Se Josh non fosse stato in grado di assistere all'operazione, avrebbe aspettato in camera sua. Ero certo però che non se ne sarebbe andato prima di essere convinto che Gavin era guarito.

Presi il telecomando, e stavo per premere il tasto quando sentii uno strattone al polso che quasi me lo fece cadere di mano.

"Papà!" esclamò Josh allarmato. "Ma cosa stai facendo?"

Abbassai il telecomando e mi accosciai per guardarlo faccia a faccia. Gli mostrai il telecomando, indicando che era simile a ogni altro dispositivo dalle stesse funzioni che avevamo in casa.

"È solo per spegnerlo mentre lo aggiusto" risposi.

Josh sembrava preso dal panico.

"Morirà?"

La sua voce era un mormorio strozzato che mi colpì come un pugno nello stomaco.

"No" risposi pacatamente. "Una volta aggiustato, lo riaccenderò. Esattamente come quando riaccendi il computer o il televisore".

Il che non era poi tanto lontano dalla verità …

La mia spiegazione sembrò rassicurarlo, ma non del tutto.

"Allora è come se rimane addormentato mentre lo aggiusti?"

"Esatto" dissi. "Un po' come quando ti hanno tolto le tonsille. Ti sei addormentato mentre il dottore ti operava, e poi ti sei svegliato".

Josh fece una smorfia. "Non mi è piaciuto per niente" disse. "È stato disgustoso. E la gola mi faceva male".

Sorrisi e gli misi la mano sulla spalla. "Lo so".

Non era piaciuto neanche a me vedere soffrire mio figlio e non poter fare nulla.

Gli presi la mano. "Non sarà così per Gavin" lo rassicurai. "Non è capace di sentire dolore." "Almeno non come lo sentiamo noi" aggiunsi subito.

Josh guardò Gavin. "È per quello che non piange?"

"Sì" risposi, sollevato di vedere che Josh capiva.

Josh studiò il viso di Gavin, mentre gli occhi del fratellino seguivano i suoi movimenti.

"Sognerà?"

Gettai un'occhiata a Gavin, immobile sul banco da lavoro. Anche lui sembrava aspettasse la mia risposta.

"Credo di no".

Devo ammettere che non ero del tutto certo. Spento, sarebbe diventato nient'altro che un insieme di componenti elettronici, quindi senza consapevolezza di sé. L'unica differenza sarebbe stata che, quando si fosse 'risvegliato', la sincronizzazione dei suoi orologi interni sarebbe stata alterata.

Josh sembrava profondamente preoccupato.

"E se non riesci a risvegliarlo?"

Mentre lo avevo costruito, avevo probabilmente spento e riacceso Gavin più di un centinaio di volte, sempre senza alcun problema. Quelle poche volte che non si era riacceso subito erano state quasi tutte dovute a errori da me commessi; errori dai quali avevo imparato, sicché non vedevo nessuna ragione per cui l'operazione di riparare il braccio non dovesse essere un successo. Ma era anche vero che qualcosa poteva sempre andar male senza un motivo discernibile.

Con un sorriso inteso a rincuorarlo, misi di nuovo la mano sulla spalla di Josh.

"Una volta riparato, dovrebbe risvegliarsi senza problemi".

"Nonno John non si è risvegliato" disse Josh sottovoce, profondamente impensierito.

Il mio sorriso svanì, e la mia mano si strinse sulla sua spalla.

"Lo so" risposi quietamente. "Ma Nonno John era molto vecchio … e alle persone vecchie a volte capita. Gavin non è vecchio".

Era vero che dal punto di vista cronologico Gavin aveva solo pochi mesi — se vogliamo considerare la data di attivazione come la sua "data di nascita". Dal punto di vista dello sviluppo … beh, non ci avevo mai pensato. Fisicamente sembrava un po' più giovane di Josh. E se qualcuno dei suoi componenti si fosse consumato o avesse avuto bisogno di riparazioni — ad esempio il suo braccio — avrei potuto …

Quando me ne resi conto, fui stupito di non averci mai pensato. Con tutto ciò che avevo letto e imparato, avrebbe dovuto venirmi in mente molto tempo prima.

"Sai una cosa?" risposi eccitato. "Finché si trovano i componenti per ripararlo, non vedo perché non potrebbe vivere praticamente per sempre".

"Davvero?"

Josh sembrava molto impressionato, ma ero certo che nei suoi luminosi occhi azzurri c'era anche dello scetticismo.

Stavo per rispondere, poi rimasi in silenzio e decisi di non svelare per il momento le implicazioni della mia scoperta. Cominciavo solo allora a capirle a fondo, e temevo che non sarei stato in grado di spiegarle a Josh in maniera soddisfacente.

Josh guardava Gavin; e avrei potuto giurare che Gavin guardava lui con un'espressione di completa fiducia e comprensione.

"Fidati di me" dissi con calma. "Andrà tutto bene".

Josh ancora non sembrava del tutto convinto.

Non sapevo cos'altro aggiungere. *Forse è così che si sentono i chirurghi prima di entrare in sala operatoria,* pensai.

"Vuoi dirglielo tu?" gli chiesi, indicando Gavin.

Josh spalancò gli occhi. Fece cenno di no, ancora più impaurito.

Mi rialzai e mi avvicinai al banco da lavoro. Mi concentrai su tutto ciò che non faceva di Gavin un bambino vero: la parrucca, la pelle di plastica, il braccio contorto in posizione innaturale. Mi fu d'aiuto, ma non tanto.

"Adesso ti spegnerò per un po" gli dissi "per aggiustarti il braccio". Feci una pausa, non sapendo se Gavin mi avrebbe davvero dato una risposta. "Va bene?"

Gavin semplicemente batté gli occhi. Mi chiesi se forse i suoi sistemi audio erano danneggiati. Finora non aveva detto una parola o emesso un suono.

"D'accordo?" ripetei, aggrottando la fronte.

Dalla bocca di Gavin uscì un suono roco, quasi inaudibile.

"Sì".

Premetti il tasto del telecomando.

Quasi tutte le attività visualizzate sul monitor calarono a zero. L'unico cambiamento esterno era che Gavin non batteva più gli occhi. Gli occhi rimanevano aperti, ma sapevo che avevano cessato di ricevere dati. In uno strano senso sembrava che la sua anima fosse volata via.

Mi ripromisi che avrei fatto solo il minimo necessario. Distolsi lo sguardo, il che mi costò molta più forza di volontà di quanto avrei potuto immaginare, e vidi che Josh stava lottando contro le lacrime. Gli misi una mano sulla spalla.

"Andrà tutto bene" lo rassicurai. "Va' a farti uno spuntino. Mi ci vorrà del tempo per aggiustarlo".

Pensai che Josh avrebbe protestato. Osservò Gavin a lungo, poi si allontanò riluttante e salì le scale, diretto in cucina.

Devo confessare che aggiustare il braccio di Gavin fu meno facile e meno rapido di quanto pensassi. Riuscii a completare l'operazione con pezzi di ricambio che mi ritrovavo sottomano, ma qua e là dovetti improvvisare. Dall'esterno nessuno probabilmente avrebbe notato nulla; decisi che bastava, perché sarebbe bastato a Josh.

Non mi ero accorto che Josh era silenziosamente tornato nel seminterrato. Sedeva sulle scale, sgranocchiando delle noccioline e osservandomi mentre lavoravo. Non so se osservare l'intera operazione calmasse le sue paure, ma non si mosse da dov'era finché non terminai il lavoro.

Quando fui finalmente pronto a riattivare Gavin, guardai il telecomando, pronto a premere il tasto; poi invece feci cenno a Josh di venirmi accanto. "Vuoi farlo tu?"

Josh apparve stupito. Gettò una cauta occhiata al telecomando, poi a me. Aspettai, dandogli il tempo di decidere, consapevole che così stavo affidando a lui il potere di controllare il fratellino a volontà.

Alla fine si decise. Non prese il telecomando ma spinse il tasto con un movimento improvviso dell'indice, poi subito ritrasse la mano come se il tasto lo avesse punto.

Un attimo dopo udimmo il suono rassicurante di Gavin che si risvegliava. Il momento più rassicurante di tutti fu quando Gavin ricominciò a battere gli occhi. Volse la testa e fermò lo sguardo su Josh. Emisi un lungo sospiro di sorpresa e di sollievo.

Josh mi guardò con un sorriso trionfante.

"Grazie, papà!"

Sorrisi anch'io, molto soddisfatto di me stesso.

"Di nulla, giovanotto. Vuoi che lo porto su?"

"No, posso farlo io" rispose Josh, con un padronanza di sé che mi fece sorridere.

"Bene, allora andiamo ".

Misi Gavin a sedere sul banco da lavoro. Gavin sollevò entrambe le braccia, Josh se lo mise a cavalluccio, e insieme si avviarono verso la scala, intrepidi.

Riposi i miei attrezzi. *A volte* — mi dissi felice — *papà può ancora aggiustare tutto.*

5

Q UALCHE GIORNO DOPO, mentre passavo davanti alla stanza di Josh con il cesto della biancheria sottobraccio, mi soffermai a dare un'occhiata.

Josh e Gavin erano intenti a bombardare astronavi sullo schermo del televisore in un'epica battaglia galattica. Sorrisi nostalgico, ricordando la mia infanzia. Josh e io avevamo trascorso molte ore intenti a quel videogioco, cercando di sconfiggere le forze dell'impero del male prima che ci facessero esplodere in mille frammenti colorati. Josh, naturalmente, era stato molto più bravo di me.

Nessuno dei due diceva una parola. Sembravano comunicare invece con una serie irregolare di sibili e borbottii quasi impercettibili. Notai che la coordinazione di Gavin era palesemente migliorata dall'ultima volta che li avevo visti giocare assieme. Ovviamente i movimenti di Josh erano molto più fluidi, ma mi sembrava che i riflessi di Gavin si fossero fatti più pronti. Gavin aveva limiti di destrezza — una funzione che non ero ancora riuscito a perfezionare — ma compensava facendo scattare le braccia e le mani verso la console con velocità meccanica molto più efficace di quella umana.

Josh distolse l'attenzione per un istante. Mi vide sull'uscio, e sorrise. Sorrisi anch'io. Mi rallegrò il cuore vedere che anche con la presenza di Gavin, rimanevo una parte importante del mondo di mio figlio.

"Ciao papà" disse allegramente Josh. "Vuoi venire a guardare?"

"Certo".

Lasciai il cesto della biancheria nel corridorio ed entrai, cercando di non calpestare giocattoli assortiti sparsi sulla moquette. Trovai uno spazio libero e mi sedetti a terra.

Osservai a lungo i due bambini. Pilotavano le loro astronavi in tandem, con perizia. Uno manovrava la propria per intrappolare le astronavi nemiche, l'altro le faceva esplodere. Di quando in quando si scambiavano i ruoli, sempre senza dirsi una parola.

Se diventano veri piloti — mi dissi — *una dozzina di nazioni sulla terra farebbe bene ad arrendersi subito.*

Per tutto il tempo che rimasi nella stanza, nessuno dei due mi rivolse la parola. Li osservavo progredire da un livello all'altro di difficoltà del gioco, e mi sentii prendere da una profonda tristezza. Riflettei per qualche minuto, con onesta introspezione, sul perché. Infine capii: in un arco di tempo di appena poche settimane, Josh era passato da "Papà, vuoi giocare?" a "Papà, vuoi guardare?"

Da quando avevo attivato Gavin, Josh ed io avevamo trascorso molto meno tempo insieme. Avevo permesso che Gavin diventasse il mio sostituto. Lo usavo per intrattenere Josh, per poter avere più tempo libero in cui dedicarmi ai miei progetti. Costruendo Gavin, avevo creato con le mie stesse mani un surrogato che aveva preso il mio posto in alcuni aspetti della vita di mio figlio; solo adesso mi rendevo conto di quanto quegli aspetti mi fossero cari.

Pur intento al gioco, però, ogni tanto Josh mi lanciava un'occhiata, il che mi indicava che la mia presenza non gli era sgradita; anzi, sembrava rassicurato di vedermi là. Ne fui rincuorato. Sapevo da molto che un giorno non sarei più stato la prima persona la cui compagnia mio figlio avrebbe cercato; ma avevo immaginato che sarebbe accaduto più tardi — forse quando Josh avrebbe cominciato a frequentare le scuole medie. Certo non adesso.

"Papà?"

La voce sommessa di Josh mi strappò dalla mia meditazione.

Lo guardai, con lo sguardo offuscato dalle lacrime. Cercai di asciugarmi gli occhi senza che lui lo notasse.

"C'è qualcosa che non va?" mi chiese.

Posò la console del videogioco e si chinò verso di me con aria preoccupata.

"No, va tutto bene" risposi in un sussurro. Mi schiarii la gola, cercando di ritrovare la compostezza.

Josh non sembrava persuaso. Sorrisi per convincerlo. Josh mi scrutò ancora per qualche attimo — non so se il mio sorriso riuscì a convincerlo — poi riprese a giocare.

Tirai un lungo sospiro. Josh e Gavin, i due piloti provetti, erano tornati alla loro battaglia intergalattica. Mi alzai, con l'intenzione di scusarmi perché dovevo tornare alle mie faccende domestiche; poi notai una cosa che non mi fu chiara subito: alcune delle astronavi che partecipavano al videogioco mi erano nuove. Dapprima pensai provenissero da un livello superiore di gioco che io e Josh non avevamo mai raggiunto (non ho mai detto che ci sapevamo fare da maestri). Un istante dopo non potei fare a meno di sgranare gli occhi.

Non avevo mai visto quelle astronavi in *quel* videogioco. Provenivano da tutto un altro universo immaginario. Fu una scoperta al tempo stesso inquietante e affascinante. Era un po' come se nel "Mago di Oz" al posto del Leone Codardo fosse improvvisamente apparso il leone Aslan delle "Cronache di Narnia".

"Josh?" chiesi, con la voce che quasi mi tremava. "Da dove provengono quelle astronavi?"

"Le abbiamo fatte noi" rispose Josh, senza distrarre lo sguardo dallo schermo.

Cercai di elaborare quella rivelazione. *Fatte?*

"In che modo?"

"Con il mio computer".

Guardai la console dei videogiochi, ma già sapevo che Josh non intendeva dire quella. Josh conosceva la differenza fra la console e il computer che teneva sulla sua scrivania.

Aggrottai profondamente la fronte.

"In che modo le avete fatte?"

"Le ha fatte Gavin", rispose Josh con una scrollata di spalle, come se fosse una cosa del tutto normale.

Gavin ha fatto le astronavi?

Mi misi a sedere.

"In che modo le ha fatte?"

Cercai di rimanere calmo, ma dovevo lottare contro l'impulso di allungare la mano, spegnere lo schermo ed esigere spiegazioni.

"Con quel sito che mi hai fatto vedere" rispose Josh, lievemente esasperato. "Il sito con gli indizi per i giochi".

Ora mi era tutto chiaro. Emisi un sospiro di sollievo.

Qualche tempo prima avevo evidenziato per Josh un sito in cui si potevano trovare indizi per proseguire il gioco, in caso rimanesse bloccato ad un ostacolo. Non l'avrei definito barare; avevo attivato il controllo dei genitori, sicché era necessario che Josh mi chiedesse prima il permesso di accedervi. (Confesso di aver usato il sito io stesso. Alcuni di quei videogiochi sono *difficili*).

Sul sito si potevano trovare anche dei programmi scaricabili, dei quali non mi fidavo del tutto per via del pericolo onnipresente di virus nascosti. Vari di quei programmi, però, offrivano modifiche addizionali; alcune erano permesse dagli ideatori dei giochi; altre, per validi motivi, erano vietate.

Gavin ha fatto le astronavi.

Ridacchiai fra me, ma un po' impensierito che Josh stesse cercando di addossare la colpa al fratellino se io mi fossi arrabbiato. Sapevo per esperienza personale che era una tattica ben usata tra fratelli. Josh però era figlio unico, non aveva mai avuto l'opportunità di usarla prima di allora.

Ma è una tattica innocua, decisi.

Non era quindi la console dei videogiochi che s'era inceppata. Né, da quanto potevo notare, Josh e Gavin avevano scaricato programmi dal contenuto sospetto (benché presi nota mentalmente di controllare più tardi).

Diedi un'ultima occhiata allo schermo, e a quell'inattesa fusione di due universi fantascientifici, poi uscii, scuotendo il capo tra me con un sorriso divertito. Qualche giorno dopo, mentre passavo davanti alla stanza di Josh con il cesto della biancheria sottobraccio, mi soffermai a dare un'occhiata.

Josh e Gavin erano intenti a bombardare astronavi sullo schermo del televisore in un'epica battaglia galattica. Sorrisi nostalgico, ricordando la mia infanzia. Josh e io avevamo trascorso molte ore intenti a quel videogioco, cercando di sconfiggere le forze dell'impero del male prima che ci facessero esplodere in mille frammenti colorati. Josh, naturalmente, era stato molto più bravo di me.

Nessuno dei due diceva una parola. Sembravano comunicare invece con una serie irregolare di sibili e borbottii quasi impercettibili. Notai che la coordinazione di Gavin era palesemente migliorata dall'ultima volta che li avevo visti giocare assieme. Ovviamente i movimenti di Josh erano molto più fluidi, ma mi sembrava che i riflessi di Gavin si fossero fatti più pronti. Gavin aveva limiti di destrezza — una funzione che non ero ancora riuscito a perfezionare — ma compensava facendo scattare le braccia e le mani verso la console con velocità meccanica molto più efficace di quella umana.

Josh distolse l'attenzione per un istante. Mi vide sull'uscio, e sorrise. Sorrisi anch'io. Mi rallegrò il cuore vedere che anche con la presenza di Gavin, rimanevo una parte importante del mondo di mio figlio.

"Ciao papà" disse allegramente Josh. "Vuoi venire a guardare?"

"Certo".

Lasciai il cesto della biancheria nel corridorio ed entrai, cercando di non calpestare giocattoli assortiti sparsi sulla moquette. Trovai uno spazio libero e mi sedetti a terra.

Osservai a lungo i due bambini. Pilotavano le loro astronavi in tandem, con perizia. Uno manovrava la propria per intrappolare le astronavi nemiche, l'altro le faceva esplodere. Di quando in quando si scambiavano i ruoli, sempre senza dirsi una parola.

Se diventano veri piloti — mi dissi — *una dozzina di nazioni sulla terra farebbe bene ad arrendersi subito.*

Per tutto il tempo che rimasi nella stanza, nessuno dei due mi rivolse la parola. Li osservavo progredire da un livello all'altro di difficoltà del gioco, e mi sentii prendere da una profonda tristezza. Riflettei per qualche minuto, con onesta introspezione, sul perché. Infine capii: in un arco di tempo di appena poche settimane, Josh era passato da "Papà, vuoi giocare?" a "Papà, vuoi guardare?"

Da quando avevo attivato Gavin, Josh ed io avevamo trascorso molto meno tempo insieme. Avevo permesso che Gavin diventasse il mio sostituto. Lo usavo per intrattenere Josh, per poter avere più tempo libero in cui dedicarmi ai miei progetti. Costruendo Gavin, avevo creato con le mie stesse mani un surrogato che aveva preso il mio posto in alcuni aspetti della vita di mio figlio; solo adesso mi rendevo conto di quanto quegli aspetti mi fossero cari.

Pur intento al gioco, però, ogni tanto Josh mi lanciava un'occhiata, il che mi indicava che la mia presenza non gli era sgradita; anzi, sembrava rassicurato di vedermi là. Ne fui rincuorato. Sapevo da molto che un giorno non sarei più stato la prima persona la cui compagnia mio figlio avrebbe cercato; ma avevo immaginato che sarebbe accaduto più tardi — forse quando Josh avrebbe cominciato a frequentare le scuole medie. Certo non adesso.

"Papà?"

La voce sommessa di Josh mi strappò dalla mia meditazione.

Lo guardai, con gli occhi affuscati dalle lacrime. Cercai di asciugarmi gli occhi senza che lui lo notasse.

"C'è qualcosa che non va?" mi chiese.

Posò la console del videogioco e si chinò verso di me con aria preoccupata.

"No, va tutto bene" risposi in un sussurro. Mi schiarii la gola, cercando di ritrovare la compostezza.

Josh non sembrava persuaso. Sorrisi per convincerlo. Josh mi scrutò ancora per qualche attimo — non so se il mio sorriso riuscì a convincerlo — poi riprese a giocare.

Tirai un lungo sospiro. Josh e Gavin, i due piloti provetti, erano tornati alla loro battaglia intergalattica. Mi alzai, con l'intenzione di scusarmi perché dovevo tornare alle mie faccende domestiche; poi notai una cosa che non mi fu chiara subito: alcune delle astronavi che partecipavano al videogioco mi erano nuove. Dapprima pensai provenissero da un livello superiore di gioco che io e Josh non avevamo mai raggiunto (non ho mai detto che ci sapevamo fare da maestri). Un istante dopo non potei fare a meno di sgranare gli occhi.

Non avevo mai visto quelle astronavi in quel videogioco. Provenivano da tutto un altro universo immaginario. Fu una scoperta al tempo stesso inquietante e affascinante. Era un po' come se nel "Mago di Oz" al posto del Leone Codardo fosse improvvisamente apparso il leone Aslan delle "Cronache di Narnia".

"Josh?" chiesi, con la voce che quasi mi tremava. "Da dove provengono quelle astronavi?"

"Le abbiamo fatte noi" rispose Josh, senza distrarre lo sguardo dallo schermo.

Cercai di elaborare quella rivelazione. *Fatte?*

"In che modo?"

"Con il mio computer".

Guardai la console dei videogiochi, ma già sapevo che Josh non intendeva dire quella. Josh conosceva la differenza fra la console e il computer che teneva sulla sua scrivania.

Aggrottai profondamente la fronte.

"In che modo le avete fatte?"

"Le ha fatte Gavin", rispose Josh con una scrollata di spalle, come se fosse una cosa del tutto normale.

Gavin ha fatto le astronavi?

Mi misi a sedere.

"In che modo le ha fatte?"

Cercai di rimanere calmo, ma dovevo lottare contro l'impulso di allungare la mano, spegnere lo schermo ed esigere spiegazioni.

"Con quel sito che mi hai fatto vedere" rispose Josh, lievemente esasperato. "Il sito con gli indizi per i giochi".

Ora mi era tutto chiaro. Emisi un sospiro di sollievo.

Qualche tempo prima avevo evidenziato per Josh un sito in cui si potevano trovare indizi per proseguire il gioco, in caso rimanesse bloccato ad un ostacolo. Non l'avrei definito barare; avevo attivato il controllo dei genitori, sicché era necessario che Josh mi chiedesse prima il permesso di accedervi. (Confesso di aver usato il sito io stesso. Alcuni di quei videogiochi sono *difficili*).

Sul sito si potevano trovare anche dei programmi scaricabili, dei quali non mi fidavo del tutto per via del pericolo onnipresente di virus nascosti. Vari di quei programmi, però, offrivano modifiche addizionali; alcune erano permesse dagli ideatori dei giochi, altre, per validi motivi, erano vietate.

Gavin ha fatto le astronavi.

Ridacchiai fra me, ma un po' impensierito che Josh stesse cercando di addossare la colpa al fratellino se io mi fossi arrabbiato. Sapevo per esperienza personale che era una tattica ben usata tra fratelli. Josh però era figlio unico, non aveva mai avuto l'opportunità di usarla prima di allora.

Ma è una tattica innocua, decisi.

Non era quindi la console dei videogiochi che s'era inceppata. Né, da quanto potevo notare, Josh e Gavin avevano scaricato programmi dal contenuto sospetto (benché presi nota mentalmente di controllare più tardi).

Diedi un'ultima occhiata allo schermo, e a quell'inattesa fusione di due universi fantascientifici, poi uscii, scuotendo il capo tra me con un sorriso divertito.

6

MOLTO TEMPO DOPO CHE JOSH SI FU ADDORMENTATO, andai a sedermi nel mio laboratorio del seminterrato. Non riuscivo a dormire; c'era qualcosa che mi turbava, ma non sapevo cosa. Mentre osservavo gli strumenti con i quali avevo dato vita a Gavin, per la prima volta venni colpito dalle implicazioni di quanto avevo creato.

Non era tanto l'aspetto tecnico, benché esso fosse di per sé degno di nota. C'erano probabilmente una mezza dozzina di brevetti che avrei potuto richiedere in base alla mia opera. Ammesso, ovviamente, che non ne avessi infranto alcuni già esistenti.

No, decisi poi fermamente. *Si tratta d'altro ... qualcosa di molto più profondo.*

Avevo creato Gavin perché fosse un compagno più o meno consapevole per Josh. Lo avevo programmato in modo che potesse ascoltare le istruzioni di Josh, valutarle, e reagire come meglio poteva. A dire il vero, lo avevo programmato in modo che ascoltasse le istruzioni di qualunque — in particolar modo le mie. Era anche in grado di analizzare e archiviare le reazioni ricevute, e di farne uso per migliorare le sue interazioni future. Insomma lo avevo programmato perché fosse in grado di *imparare* e, a quanto pareva, aveva imparato.

Cos'altro aveva imparato? mi chiesi. *E quali conclusioni aveva tratto da ciò che aveva imparato, da tutti quei dati che aveva raccolto?*

Ero divorato dalla curiosità. Dovevo assolutamente scoprirlo.

Mi accertai che Josh dormisse, poi accesi Gavin in modalità pausa. Si sarebbe svegliato e avrebbe reagito solo se io mi fossi rivolto direttamente a lui, ma avrebbe cessato di elaborare ogni altro dato. Dopodiché cominciai a scaricare una copia dei suoi dati interni su unità non direttamente collegate ai suoi sistemi informatici. Mentre aspettavo che venisse completato lo scaricamento, mi misi alla ricerca dei dati che Gavin aveva scelto di archiviare nella sua memoria permanente.

Scoprii che il suo sistema di archiviazione era rimasto praticamente inalterato da come lo avevo progettato. Vi trovai innanzitutto cartelle riservate alle persone con le quali aveva interagito a cominciare dal momento in cui era stato attivato: io, Josh e Carolyn. Quest'ultimo dato mi sorprese. A quanto mi constava, le interazioni fra Carolyn e Gavin erano consistite in appena qualche saluto scambiato più che altro su insistenza di Josh. Inoltre, Carolyn si era sempre categoricamente rifiutata di permettere che Josh portasse Gavin con sé quando lei e Josh trascorrevano il fine settimana assieme, benché Josh la implorasse ogni volta (ero stato io a persuadere più o meno Josh che per il momento era meglio che Gavin rimanesse un nostro piccolo segreto di famiglia).

Scoprii inoltre che Gavin aveva creato varie cartelle dedicate alla conservazione di dati riguardanti categorie particolari. Alcune di queste erano da prevedersi, ad esempio dati sul suo ambiente e procedure necessarie a portare a termine compiti di un certo genere.

Comprese tecniche di videogiochi, notai sorridendo fra me.

I titoli enigmatici che Gavin aveva dato a queste nuove cartelle mi facevano infuriare, benché a dire il vero me lo aspettassi. Anni di esperienza mi avevano abituato a titoli di cartelle apparentemente assegnati in base a sequenze del tutto casuali.

Spinto dalla curiosità, ma esitante, mi misi a sondare il contenuto delle cartelle. Il lato pignolo di me voleva convincermi che ciò era un'invasione della vita privata di Gavin, né più né meno che leggere la sua posta elettronica a sua insaputa. Mi ci volle un po' per azzittire quella vocina da grillo parlante. Ciononostante, mi rendevo conto che essa era non solo un rimprovero ma anche un avvertimento. Alla fine la misi a tacere rammentando a me stesso che Gavin non era una persona reale, che era come esaminare il contenuto di qualunque altra banca dati.

Funzionò. Più o meno.

Dapprima fui leggermente deluso da quanto scoprii. Erano solo dati, informazioni frammentarie che Gavin aveva archiviato a partire dal momento in cui era stato attivato per la prima volta. Poi, mentre continuavo la ricerca, il mio stato d'animo cominciò a mutare. È demoralizzante — e non poco inquietante — vedere le proprie reazioni emotive ridotte a conglomerati di statistiche. Alcuni dei dati erano ovviamente contraddittori, ma da quanto potevo vedere, la maggior parte delle conclusioni raggiunte da Gavin era rigorosamente corretta.

Mi mortificò apprendere ad esempio che, a detta di Gavin, quando non ero con Josh mi vestivo in prevalenza di grigio. Sempre secondo Gavin, quando la madre di Josh lo portava da me, lei si vestiva in prevalenza di varie tonalità di viola. A dire il vero erano colori che le donavano, ma non portava sempre quelli, e Gavin apparentemente non era ancora riuscito a correlare uno schema. Dalle conclusioni che avevo raggiunto io, l'abbigliamento di Carolyn dipendeva da cosa accadeva nel suo lavoro in quel giorno particolare. Il venerdì informale dell'ufficio, ad esempio, per lei non era mai informale.

Dalla bocca dei bambini esce la verità …

O in questo caso, mi corressi dentro di me, *dalla mente algoritmica di un bambino artificiale …*

Quali altre percezioni, mi chiesi, *si annidavano nella memoria permanente di Gavin?*

Continuai a sondare sempre più a fondo il contenuto delle cartelle, al tempo stesso affascinato e atterrito.

Forse è questo che uno prova quando ha la telepatia, il potere di spalancare la mente altrui …

Proseguendo le mie indagini, scoprii un archivio il cui scopo dapprima non riuscii a identificare. Il formato di base non rivelava nulla, ma quello me l'aspettavo; avrei trovato un sistema per accedere. Il non poter accedervi facilmente aumentava però la mia curiosità. Dopo vari tentativi a vuoto, quando stavo per arrendermi alla stanchezza, finalmente mi resi conto che i dati delle cartelle erano inaccessibili perché nascosti in profondità.

Perché Gavin nasconde dati? mi stupii con un brivido. Non ricordavo di avere incluso protocolli di crittografia nei suoi programmi operativi. Forse li avevo inclusi all'inizio e poi me n'ero dimenticato perché non avevo mai pensato che Gavin avrebbe avuto motivo di utilizzarli. Era però anche vero che non gli avevo mai *proibito* di utilizzarli.

Mi sentii prendere dal panico.

Segreti, pensai. *Gavin aveva segreti.*

Provai un certo sollievo nel vedere che le cartelle sigillate erano relativamente poche. Il che voleva dire che Josh non aveva rivelato al fratellino tutti i suoi segreti. Certo non glieli avevo rivelati io. Cercai di ricordare se nelle settimane trascorse io avessi mai chiesto a Gavin di mantenere un segreto. Senz'altro un paio di volte dovevo aver detto ad entrambi qualcosa come "… ma non dirlo alla tua mamma, d'accordo?"

Lo avevo inteso come una battuta innocente, probabilmente per nascondere qualche mia piccola infrazione che Carolyn non avrebbe approvato — ad esempio dare a Josh una ciotola di gelato al posto di un pasto nutriente.

Ma Gavin era in grado solo di interpretare la mia frase come un ordine, di registrare il dato alla lettera e di conservarlo al sicuro nell'unica maniera di cui era capace.

Una cosa avevo imparato da tutto quel tempo trascorso a leggere fantascienza: quando un'intelligenza artificiale comincia a nascondere cose — in special modo al suo creatore — il più delle volte non è un buon segno.

Benché sorpreso, cercai di allontanare i miei dubbi con ragionamenti di vario genere. Forse ero ingenuo, forse ero di parte nei confronti della mia creazione, ma mi rifiutavo di credere che ci fosse un intento malizioso nella sua decisione di nascondere dati. Gavin aveva seguito le istruzioni ricevute, tutto qua. Dove non gli avevo fornito programmi atti a gestire questo genere di situazione, ne aveva inventato di propri. C'era anzi da esserne colpiti.

Ma il dubbio non svaniva.

In quali circostanze Gavin avrebbe scelto di mentire? Era capace di mentire, o di non rivelare la verità? In base a quali criteri si sarebbe regolato nel decidere che la segretezza era la scelta corretta?

A quanto mi constava, Gavin non si era mai trovato in quella situazione. O, se vi si era trovato, fra le varie opzioni aveva scelto il silenzio. Non avevo programmato la mia creazione per mentire; né, mi resi conto solo allora, gli avevo imposto di dire sempre la verità. Se Gavin aveva mai mentito, non lo avevo colto sul fatto. Josh non ne aveva mai parlato, ma forse perché non gli era mai venuto in mente di parlarne. Sapevo bene che condividere segreti era una cosa molto comune tra fratelli. Nel caso di Gavin, però ...

Potrei risolvere il problema, mi dissi. *Potrei aggiornare i suoi programmi in modo tale che debba dire sempre la verità. Sarebbe un compito facilissimo.*

Le mani mi rimasero sospese sulla tastiera. No, non potevo farlo. Se lo avessi fatto avrei alterato in maniera irrevocabile il comportamento di Gavin — l'essenza di Gavin.

Guardavo lo schermo del computer come inebetito. La mia mente si rifiutava di mettere assieme altri pensieri.

Gettai un'occhiata all'orologio: era molto più tardi di quanto pensassi. Con un sospiro di rassegnata stanchezza, spensi lo schermo. Come sempre, Gavin si sarebbe "svegliato" fra qualche ora, assieme a Josh. Intanto avevo bisogno di riposo. Forse nel sonno sarei riuscito a trovare le risposte.

Non ci contavo granché.

7

LA MATTINA DOPO, mentre Josh era a scuola, portai Gavin nel mio laboratorio del seminterrato. Era l'ora ideale per apportare le mie modifiche, ancor più di quando Josh dormiva. Se qualcosa fosse andato male — e a volte andava male, ogni tanto in maniera considerevole — Josh non ne sarebbe stato testimone. Ciò che però mi premeva stavolta era parlare con Gavin.

Lo deposi sul mio banco da lavoro e lo collegai ai sistemi di monitoraggio. Stavolta però attivai ogni opzione che mi permetteva di controllare il registro attività di Gavin nei minimi dettagli. Più in là lo avrei studiato per scoprire quali sottoprogrammi usava per conversare con me. I sottoprogrammi mi avrebbero anche consentito di vedere non solo i dati ai quali Josh aveva avuto accesso ma, il che era ancora più importante, anche i dati che aveva deciso di non conservare oppure di nascondere quando gli facevo domande. Mi resi conto che in sostanza lo stavo collegando a una macchina della verità.

Provai un profondo senso di colpa, ma misi a tacere la voce sommessa della mia coscienza. Sapevo che si sarebbe ripresentata più tardi, che forse mi avrebbe perfino perseguitato nei sogni. Al tempo stesso, ero convinto che quello era l'unico mezzo per porre fine ai miei dubbi.

Dopo aver osservato Gavin per alcuni minuti, mi ritrovai del tutto incerto su come cominciare.

Sembra così facile in televisione.

Gavin giaceva supino sul banco da lavoro, anche lui osservandomi in silenzio. I suoi occhi mi seguivano mentre armeggiavo qua e là futilmente. Ero perfettamente cosciente di non stare concludendo nulla tranne che procrastinare.

Mi fermai davanti a lui, cercando di assumere un atteggiamento deciso ma neutrale.

"Gavin?"

I suoi occhi si posarono sul mio volto.

Era ancora inquietante, dopo tanto tempo, quando mi fissava a quel modo. Carolyn mi aveva detto più d'una volta che le dava i brividi. A Josh però non dava mai fastidio. E io preferivo non fare commenti.

Finalmente decisi che mi stava prestando completa attenzione, benché sapessi che non era del tutto vero.

"Voglio farti alcune domande" presi a dire. "Solo per controllare alcuni dei tuoi sistemi", aggiunsi subito.

Sono certo che Gavin aveva notato il mio goffo tentativo di ingannarlo. Ma proseguii.

"D'accordo" rispose blando.

Mi ci volle un attimo per rendermi conto che probabilmente Gavin intendeva dimostrarmi che era una perdita di tempo, esattamente come avrebbe fatto un vero bambino nella stessa situazione. Ma non mutò espressione e non mosse gli occhi, tranne che per aprirli e chiuderli con quel ritmo irregolare che avevo programmato.

Nonostante avessi provato mentalmente più volte la conversazione, ero riluttante a intraprenderla.

Di cosa avevo paura? mi chiesi. *Di scoprire ciò che già sospettavo era vero?*

Studiai il piccolo corpo vestito degli indumenti che avevo scelto per lui. Sapevo cosa coprivano, ma una parte di me si rifiutava di crederlo. L'illusione stava diventando reale.

Infine tirai un profondo sospiro e cominciai.

"Come ti chiami?

"Gavin" rispose con voce piatta.

"Come mi chiamo?

"Papà."

Lo disse senza tono, senza il minimo cenno di affetto.

"Perché mi chiami così e non con il mio nome?"

"Perché Josh ti chiama così. Non mi hai dato istruzioni di chiamarti in altro modo".

Aggrottai la fronte, cercando d'ignorare un'improvvisa, dolorosa fitta di delusione. La risposta era quasi del tutto vera. Quando avevo creato Gavin, non c'era stato bisogno che mi chiamasse per nome; ero l'unico essere umano col quale comunicava.

"Ci sono altre ragioni?"

Mi sembrò di notare una lieve pausa prima della risposta.

"Secondo i dati ai quali ho accesso, viene generalmente considerato scortese che i figli si rivolgano ai genitori con il loro nome proprio".

Sembrava stesse recitando da un manuale.

"È vero" dissi bonariamente.

Un attimo dopo il mio sorriso svanì. Mi resi conto del significato di quanto aveva detto.

"Ti consideri uno dei miei figli?"

La risposta non fu istantanea. Battè gli occhi com'era solito fare, ma non rivelò alcun indizio su quali dati stesse elaborando. Infine mi rispose.

"Sì".

Rimasi senza parole. Era la risposta che mi aspettavo, ma chiaramente non ero pronto a sentirla.

"Perché?" chiesi con voce roca. Tutto il resto che volevo dire mi rimase come un groppo in gola.

"Mi hai creato" spiegò Gavin. "Come hai creato Josh".

Lo guardai fisso per un attimo, cercando di afferrare la frase. Poi non potei fare a meno di ridacchiare.

"Con Josh è stato un po' diverso".

"Sì".

L'umorismo presumibilmente involontario di quella singola parola non fece che aumentare la mia inquietudine.

"Gavin" dissi, tornando all'argomento che mi premeva. "Come hai imparato a modificare quel gioco?"

"Me lo ha insegnato Josh".

"Oh" mormorai. Mi aspettvo una spiegazione più profonda, più complessa.

"In che modo te lo ha insegnato?" Adesso era solo curiosità.

"Me lo ha fatto vedere sul suo computer".

"Sul suo computer?"

Aggrottai la fronte. Non mi ero mai accertato se i programmi di Gavin fossero capaci di ricevere dati in maniera indiretta.

"Sì".

"Cos'ha fatto Josh?"

"Mi ha insegnato come trovare dati usando il suo computer. Ha detto che posso usarlo per imparare molte cose, come fa lui a scuola".

"Suppongo che il computer serva a quello" dissi fra me. Poi fui colpito da un pensiero. "Hai desiderio di imparare?"

Stavolta Gavin mi rispose senza esitazione.

"Sì".

"Perché?"

"Perché mi occorrono dati".

"Perché ti occorrono dati?"

"Per soddisfare pienamente i requisiti della mia programmazione".

Mi venne un brivido. Ricordavo di aver già sentito qualcosa di simile. Anche il tono di voce proveniva dalla stessa fonte.

"In che modo?" chiesi con la gola stretta.

"Mi occorre continuare a sviluppare la mia capacità di interagire con le persone. Non posso migliorarla se non ho accesso a dati sul loro comportamento".

"Interagisci con noi" dissi, indicando la stanza di Josh al piano di sopra. "E anche molto bene", aggiunsi con un lieve sorriso.

"Sì" rispose Gavin. "Posso interagire adeguatamente con voi perché posso osservarvi. Posso formulare correlazioni fra le vostre azioni passate e il vostro comportamento previsto nelle stesse circostanze".

"Quindi non capisco qual'è il problema."

"Josh vuole farmi conoscere i suoi amici" spiegò Gavin. "In base ai dati che mi ha fornito, essi sono diversi da lui sotto molti aspetti significativi. I dati forniti non sono sufficienti a una interazione efficace con gli amici di Josh".

"Non ne sono sicuro" dissi. "Hai desiderio di conoscere i suoi amici?"

"Sì" disse subito Gavin. "Voglio adempiere alla mia programmazione".

Non era la risposta che mi aspettavo. Poi mi resi conto che aveva infatti risposto alla mia domanda.

"E per cosa sei programmato?"

"Per interagire con Josh. Per analizzare il suo comportamento in modo da poter migliorare sempre più le mie interazioni con lui". Si fermò un attimo. "Se devo interagire anche con gli amici di Josh, devo includerli nella mia analisi".

Lo guardai da vicino. La mia intenzione era stata semplicemente di creare un compagno per Josh, un giocattolo sperimentale e nient'altro. Ora invece capivo che un giorno Josh non avrebbe più avuto bisogno del suo fratellino artificiale. Gavin non sarebbe cresciuto — non sarebbe *potuto* crescere — assieme a Josh. Cosa ne avrei fatto di Gavin quando sarebbe diventato un inutile pupazzo obsoleto?

Rimasi muto sotto lo sguardo inalterabile di Gavin. Anche con i dati su di me che aveva raccolto e analizzato, non credo fosse in grado di comprendere il mio disagio. Era come spiegare la morte a un bambino — ed era un argomento che non ero ancora pronto ad affrontare.

"Gavin" dissi quietamente, senza molta convinzione nella voce "per adesso è tutto".

Gavin semplicemente mi guardò; poi mi parve che facesse lievemente cenno di sì.

8

NEI GIORNI CHE SEGUIRONO, la questione del futuro di Gavin continuò a pesarmi. In qualunque cosa io fossi occupato, mi tornava sempre alla mente ciò che ci eravamo detti. Ma neanche scrutarmi la mente mi indirizzava verso una soluzione. Con sorprendente provvidenza, fu Josh che mi aiutò a trovare una risposta, sia pure parziale.

Tornando dalla scuola, mi annunciò "Papà, ho bisogno di andare in biblioteca".

Distolsi lo sguardo dal ripiano della cucina, dove gli stavo preparando la merenda.

"Perché devi andare in biblioteca?" chiesi con una certa sorpresa. Non andavamo in biblioteca con frequenza da quando Josh aveva smesso di leggere libri illustrati. "Non puoi usare il computer per trovare quello che ti serve?"

"No" mi rispose infastidito, lasciando cadere lo zainetto sul pavimento. Prese il bicchiere di latte. "Per questo compito scolastico la signora Fox vuole che usiamo *libri veri*."

Libri veri.

Fissai gli occhi sull'arancia che stavo sbucciando, per non fargli vedere che quasi scoppiavo a ridere. Invece scossi lievemente la testa fra me con silenziosa meraviglia.

Come cambiano presto le generazioni ...

"Libri veri". Alla sua età non avevo che quelli: volumi di biblioteca, enciclopedie, grossi dizionari. Per Josh e i suoi compagni di scuola, i computer e l'internet erano ordinari come lo erano stati per me le radioline a transistor e i televisori a cassettone.

"D'accordo" dissi, mettendogli davanti il piatto con gli spicchi d'arancia e dei crackers. "Ci andiamo appena finisci".

"Grazie, papà" rispose Josh con la bocca piena di briciole di crackers.

"Nessun problema" mormorai, arruffandogli i capelli.

Josh si avventava sulla merenda con l'entusiasmo di uno che digiuna da giorni.

Come temevo pensai. *Ancora un altro scatto di crescita.*

Poi presi il piatto vuoto e lo posai nel lavandino. *Fra qualche anno guiderà lui per andare in biblioteca. O forse arrivato a quel punto potrà collegarsi alla biblioteca direttamente col cervello ...*

Smisi di lavare il piatto, lasciando che l'acqua mi scorresse sulle mani.

Forse era quella la risposta.

Una risposta parziale, ma senz'altro utile nel risolvere il mio dilemma sul futuro di Gavin. I miei pensieri presero ad accavallarsi, mentre già cominciavo a pianificare l'idea.

"Papà? Tutto bene?"

La voce di Josh mi strappò al mio fantasticare. Mi guardava con la testa piegata di lato e un'espressione circospetta.

Feci una risatina, chiudendo il rubinetto.

"Tutto bene." Gli sorrisi, per nascondergli la mia improvvisa impazienza. "Sei pronto per andare?"

Quando fummo finalmente tornati dalla biblioteca, Josh prese i suoi libri e stava per avviarsi al piano di sopra, quando si fermò a guardarmi dubbioso.

"Papà, ti comporti in modo strano".

Mi chiesi se fosse bene cercare di dargli una spiegazione. Poi decisi di no, temendo che ciò avrebbe dato adito a domande alle quali non avevo risposta.

E se mi sbaglio ...

Non ero ancora pronto ad affrontare la questione. Gli sorrisi.

"Va' a fare i compiti ... con i tuoi 'libri veri'".

Josh roteò gli occhi con comica esagerazione, poi s'avviò su per le scale.

Quando fui certo che era in camera sua, scesi di fretta nel seminterrato. Mi sedetti e afferrai la tastiera collegata ai sistemi di Gavin prima ancora di accendere la luce.

Per ragioni sia di semplicità che di sicurezza, l'accesso di Gavin agli altri computer che avevamo in casa era bloccato dall'interno. Era la stessa precauzione che avevo messo in atto per il computer di Josh, per prevenire l'entrata di virus; ma nel caso di Gavin avevo bloccato anche ogni altro genere di entrata. Non mi era mai venuto in mente che Gavin avrebbe voluto *uscire* dai suoi sistemi.

Ciò che Gavin cercava — no, ciò di cui aveva bisogno — era accesso a dati che andavano al di là di quelli disponibili nella nostra rete familiare. Mi rendevo conto solo adesso di come doveva essere stato frustrante per lui dover rimanere rinchiuso nei nostri stretti confini; era come dire a un bambino che esistono le biblioteche e poi dargli accesso a meno di una dozzina di libri; come fargli credere che quelli sarebbero stati gli unici libri che avrebbe mai avuto a sua disposizione, e che avrebbe dovuto raccogliere il resto delle informazioni qua e là da brandelli di conversazioni altrui. Mi parve un'imperdonabile crudeltà. Un profondo senso di colpa s'impadronì di me.

Rimasi seduto davanti allo schermo, non sapendo che fare. L'impulso mi spingeva a rimuovere il blocco dei programmi e a dare a Gavin libero accesso a tutto ciò che desiderava; la logica mi suggeriva che occorreva valutare i rischi. Una volta che Gavin avesse avuto accesso al mondo al di là della nostra cerchia familiare, non avrei potuto fare quasi nulla per riportarlo sotto il mio controllo. Capii quanti aspetti della creazione di Gavin mi ero fatto sfuggire; cercai di vagliare a fondo le conseguenze del mio prossimo passo.

Se avessi rimosso il blocco, Gavin avrebbe avuto accesso a una valanga di dati che non sarei stato in grado di filtrare, valutare o correggere prima che lui li assorbisse. La mia sarebbe stata una decisione irrevocabile. L'unico modo per tornare indietro sarebbe stato quello di rifare tutti i suoi sistemi da zero, e non ero neanche sicuro di poterlo fare più. Anche se fosse stato possibile, ero quasi del tutto certo che ciò che si sarebbe risvegliato non sarebbe più stato Gavin.

Eppure, mentre rimanevo assorto davanti allo schermo, rimuginando domande e incognite, sapevo di aver già preso una decisione. Non si trattava solo di decidere se Gavin fosse pronto ad affrontare un mondo più vasto. Si trattava di tutt'altro: ero pronto io a lasciare che la mia creazione si avventurasse nel mondo?

Sono i momenti più difficili per ogni genitore; una di quelle pietre miliari in cui si scopre che bisogna permettere ai figli che vadano da soli, che facciano i propri sbagli e le proprie scoperte — i loro primi passi, il loro primo giorno di scuola, le proprie prime amicizie. Lo avevo fatto con Josh. Dopo Josh credevo di aver chiuso; ora dovevo invece affrontarlo daccapo con il mio figlio artificiale. Doverlo affrontare daccapo non lo rendeva più facile. Anzi, dato il modo in cui avevo creato e allevato Gavin, era ancora più arduo.

Premetti il pulsante del citofono.

"Josh?" La voce mi tremava; sperai che Josh non lo notasse.

"Papà?"

"Gavin è in camera tua?"

"Sì, è con me". Senz'altro Josh stava pensando, "E dove altro dovrebbe essere?"

"Gavin?" chiamai.

"Sì?" La voce di Gavin era piatta e mite. Stranamente, ciò calmò le mie paure.

"Per favore prova a trovare alcune informazioni che Josh ti ha fatto vedere sul suo computer qualche giorno fa".

Mi resi conto subito dopo che forse non avrebbe capito il mio comando. "Prova a trovarle tu direttamente".

"Non posso".

Con una breve sequenza di tasti, rimossi il blocco che gli impediva l'accesso. Feci un respiro profondo. Gli avevo concesso di entrare nel mondo al di fuori della nostra casa. Irrigidito dalla tensione, confermai la rimozione del blocco.

"Riprova".

Seguì un lungo silenzio; poi sentii la voce ansiosa di Josh.

"Papà? Credo ci sia qualcosa che non va … Gavin non parla".

Controllai i monitor. Tutto sembrava a posto.

"D'accordo, Josh" risposi, cercando di mantenere la calma. "Arrivo subito".

Controllai di nuovo i monitor. Una delle schede di archiviazione lampeggiava l'allarme. Capii che Gavin avrebbe avuto bisogno di uno spazio più ampio — molto più ampio — e subito.

Quando entrai nella stanza di Josh, lo trovai che guardava a occhi spalancati Gavin, il quale era afflosciato immobile sul pavimento. Cercai parole che non sembrassero inutili o banali, ma non ci riuscii. Invece misi semplicemente la mano sulla spalla di Josh, dandogli un sorriso che voleva essere incoraggiante ma non lo era.

"Aspetta qui", sussurrai.

Mi accosciai davanti a Gavin. Gavin continuava a battere gli occhi, ma a parte quello non dava segni di notare la mia presenza.

Se non altro batte ancora gli occhi pensai, provando a rassicurare me stesso. *Non l'ho rotto del tutto.*

"Gavin?" chiesi a bassa voce. "Mi senti?" Non so perché non osavo toccarlo.

Niente. Nessun movimento, nessuna reazione. Dentro di me mi rimproverai aspramente di essere stato impaziente, di non aver aspettato che Josh andasse a dormire. Se avessi aspettato, Josh non sarebbe stato costretto a vedere il suo fratellino meccanico ridotto in quello stato.

Poi la collera e la paura presero il sopravvento. Afferrai Gavin per le spalle e lo costrinsi a guardarmi in faccia.

"Gavin, rispondimi" dissi severo, lottando per tenere sotto controllo le mie emozioni confuse.

Gavin rimase a lungo inerte. Continuava a battere gli occhi, ma la mente che avevo creato sembrava avere abbandonato il corpo al quale l'avevo collegata. D'un tratto Gavin rivolse gli occhi verso di me, facendomi sobbalzare.

"Papà". Forse era un'illusione, ma mi sembrava che i suoi occhi brillassero più di prima. Se fosse stato capace di sorridere, ero certo che avrebbe sorriso.

"C'è così tanto" disse, con una voce stranamente sommessa e cadenzata.

"Devi stare attento" dissi, soffocando le lacrime. "Non sei abituato ad assorbire tutti questi dati in una volta". Non vedevo l'ora di andare a controllare i suoi sistemi. "Non credo che tu abbia abbastanza spazio per assorbire tutto".

Avrei potuto giurare che nella sua voce ci fosse un pizzico di malinconica delusione.

"No".

Lo osservai molto attentamente. Dall'esterno sembrava del tutto normale; non notavo segni che i suoi sistemi fossero in procinto di venire meno. Volevo correre subito a verificare il funzionamento dei suoi componenti. Ma feci lo sforzo di resistere all'impulso, non volendo angosciare Josh ancora di più. *Lo farò più tardi* mi dissi *quando Josh sarà andato a dormire.*

Josh mi guardava fisso. "Gavin sta bene" gli dissi con un sorriso incerto. "Semplicemente un errore causato dalla sbadatezza di papà".

Mi alzai, dandogli un colpetto sulla spalla. "È tutto a posto" aggiunsi, cercando di sorridere con maggior convinzione. "Nulla di serio".

Josh si rilassò un poco, ma continuando a guardare il fratellino con aria preoccupata.

"Si era ammalato?

"No" risposi, scuotendo la testa. "Si era ... si era confuso per qualche minuto, tutto qui".

Almeno credo, pensai.

Cercai di convincere me stesso che Gavin non era in pericolo immediato di autodistruzione. Lasciai i due bambini a riprendere i loro giochi, pregando dentro di me che Gavin non facesse qualcos'altro di inatteso. Scesi di fretta nello scantinato, ansioso di scoprire se lo avevo danneggiato dandogli via libera di esplorare la superstrada informatica.

Iniziai la sequenza di test diagnostici che avevo programmato per monitorare la "salute" di Gavin. Come mi aspettavo, il registro attività indicava un aumento notevole. In più, adesso due delle unità dati erano quasi piene al massimo.

Collegai le due unità che tenevo di riserva, pur sapendo che era una soluzione provvisoria. Avrei dovuto acquistare unità di capacità superiore, e subito; forse non avrei potuto aspettare oltre un paio di giorni.

Mi chiesi se forse avrei dovuto costruire tutta una serie di unità separate solo per Gavin. Ciò mi avrebbe notevolmente facilitato il compito, ma prima o poi Gavin avrebbe avuto bisogno di altre unità, e poi ancora di altre ...

L'idea mi impensieriva non poco. Sapevo bene che allevare figli è costoso. Avevano sempre bisogno di qualcosa e poi di qualcos'altro. Ma non mi era mai venuto in mente che sarebbe stata la stessa cosa con un bambino meccanico. I test che stavo completando rivelavano che ogni cosa era normale. Con mio enorme sollievo, notai che le mie azioni avventate non avevano prodotto danni irreparabili; il che ovviamente non escludeva che non sarebbero emersi problemi in futuro.

Sospirai, poi allontanai la tastiera del computer e osservai l'aumento costante di attività che appariva sullo schermo. Mi chiesi come si sentiva Gavin adesso, paragonato ad appena un paio di settimane prima.

La rivelazione mi colpì. Erano davvero trascorse appena un paio di settimane? Con gli occhi fissi sul monitor, mi chiesi cosa stesse pensando Gavin.

Uno dei momenti più sconvolgenti della vita di un genitore è quello in cui si comprende che un figlio è in procinto di fare qualcosa con la quale si ha poca o nessuna dimestichezza. Non gli si può dare che consigli basati sulla propria esperienza in altri campi. In fondo, l'unica cosa che si può dire è semplicemente: "Sta' attento".

Come con i figli veri mi dissi, cercando di alleviare la mia tristezza — e senza crederci del tutto.

9

DAPPRIMA IL COMPORTAMENTO DI GAVIN cambiò in modo sottile. Alcuni dei mutamenti probabilmente mi saltarono agli occhi solo perché li cercavo. Il suo vocabolario, ad esempio, si arricchì, come pure la complessità delle sue frasi. Ovviamente Gavin aveva già avuto a disposizione dizionari, ma finora la sua scelta di espressione si era limitata a vocaboli che sentiva da noi. Un adulto con istruzione universitaria e un bambino delle elementari erano un campione circoscritto da cui apprendere l'uso del linguaggio. Perciò lo avevo programmato per reagire a comandi composti di una o massimo due parole. Adesso non era più così. Gavin era diventato capace di comprendere e di rispondere a comandi molto più lunghi e complicati.

Anche le sue conversazioni con me si erano fatte più variate. Non che Gavin fosse diventato più difficile da comprendere; ma notai che dovevo prestare maggior attenzione a quanto esprimeva, e riflettere su quanto diceva. Le sue osservazioni, già in maggior parte accurate, divennero ancora più acute e penetranti. Anzi, alcune delle nostre conversazioni mi mettevano a disagio. Non solo per via degli argomenti discussi ma anche perché adesso Gavin mi poneva domande alle quali non ero in grado di rispondere in maniera adeguata. Era come cercare di spiegare ad un alunno della scuola materna perché il cielo è azzurro o da dove vengono i bambini, senza che io stesso ne avessi un'idea precisa.

Quando le mie risposte divennero sempre meno adeguate, Gavin inevitabilmente prese a cercare risposte altrove. Non sempre trovava quelle giuste; c'è disinformazione dovunque. Eppure, gli algoritmi che aveva sviluppato per vagliare la veridicità di ciò che trovava erano incredibilmente efficaci, a volte molto più efficaci dei miei.

Ricominciai a chiedermi cosa ne facesse di tutti quei dati che raccoglieva. Ero certo che ormai doveva averne raccolto abbastanza per poter migliorare le sue interazioni con me e con Josh. Quali altre informazioni stava accumulando? E perché? Come le usava?

Finalmente un giorno glielo chiesi apertamente.

Gavin rispose in un istante.

"Imparo".

"Cosa impari?"

Stavolta ci fu una lieve esitazione.

"Tutto".

Fui colto di sorpresa. Prima che potessi rispondere, sentii squillare il telefono, il che mi costrinse a rimandare la conversazione. Me ne ricordai a notte tarda, mentre cercavo di prender sonno.

Tutto?

Nei libri che avevo letto e nei film che avevo visto, ciò non andava mai a finire bene. Mi chiesi se sarei stato capace di fermare Gavin prima che fosse troppo tardi.

Troppo tardi per cosa?

Un'altra domanda alla quale non sapevo rispondere.

10

QUALCHE SERA DOPO, mentre ero solo a leggere in salotto, udii in lontananza sirene della polizia. Benché non si sentissero spesso nella nostra zona, non vi prestai attenzione finché il loro urlare si fece sempre più vicino, poi d'improvviso si spense.

Con il libro in mano andai alla finestra. Allungando il collo notai che il trambusto proveniva dal lato della casa accanto alla nostra. Sentivo gente che gridava in vari punti della strada, ma le finestre a doppio vetro mi impedivano di capire cosa dicessero.

Con un lieve senso di colpa per la mia curiosità forse malsana, aprii appena la finestra.

"Che succede?"

Quasi mi feci cadere il libro di mano, sobbalzando. Non mi ero accorto che Josh era entrato in salotto. Mi voltai verso di lui, cercando di apparire calmo. Gli occhi di Josh erano pieni di curiosità.

"Non so" mormorai. Guardai di nuovo fuori dalla finestra. "Vedo solo auto della polizia".

"È la casa di Jeremy", disse sottovoce Josh.

Jeremy Turner abitava accanto a noi assieme ai genitori. Aveva pochi mesi meno di Josh, e come Josh era figlio unico.

Avevo incontrato varie volte sua madre, Natalie, quando portava Jeremy da noi a giocare con Josh. Mi sembrava una brava persona, benché quasi sempre un po'…. non so, ombrosa, come temesse di essere vista in compagnia di me. In genere portava vestiti di taglia inadatta e colori smorti, che sembravano scelti apposta per minimizzare la sua femminilità. Avrebbe potuto essere carina se avesse fatto uno sforzo, ma per un motivo sconosciuto preferiva non farlo.

Il padre di Jeremy, David, l'avevo incontrato sì e no un paio di volte. Non mi era mai parso un tipo socievole, anzi mi insospettiva; perciò non mi ero mai preso la briga di farmelo amico. In ogni caso, era un tipo di poche parole. Non sapevo neanche che impiego avesse. Quando usciva di casa portava un completo da lavoro, ma per quanto ne sapevo di lui, avrebbe potuto essere sia un capitano d'industria che un commesso di negozio.

A quanto dicevano i vicini, il matrimonio di Natalie e David non era rose e fiori. A giudicare dai litigi che di quando in quando sentivo provenire dalla loro casa, ero pronto a crederci. Se i due stavano litigando adesso, non avrei potuto sentirli per via del vociare delle radio della polizia.

Non ricordavo l'ultima volta che Jeremy era venuto a casa nostra a giocare con Josh. Probabilmente settimane, forse anche mesi prima.

Da quando è arrivato Gavin pensai, sentendomi un po' in colpa perché Josh aveva tralasciato Jeremy per via del fratellino meccanico.

Mi girai a guardare Josh, e mi accorsi che nei suoi occhi ora non c'era più curiosità ma paura. Lo strinsi a me, e assieme rimanemmo a spiare fra le stecche delle persiane. Non riuscivamo a distinguere nulla di quanto veniva detto fuori.

Non mi sembrava una stuazione particolarmente allarmante. Non vedevo ambulanze, pompieri, negoziatori di ostaggi o pistole estratte. Un trio di poliziotti camminava lentamente su e giù davanti alla casa dei Turner, ma nessuno dei tre con le mani sulle pistole.

Passarono lunghi minuti. Io e Josh non ci sentivamo più rilassati, anzi il fatto che non stava accadendo nulla cominciava ad innervosirci. I poliziotti continuavano ad andare pigramente su e giù, le radio delle loro auto a vociare indistinte. Poi vedemmo David Turner che usciva dalla porta d'ingresso ammanettato e scortato da altri due poliziotti.

Il riflesso delle luci delle auto si dipingeva sul suo viso a lampi alterni. Non riuscivo a interpretare la sua espressione. Camminava a testa alta, il che mi pareva sorprendente. Se fossi stato nei suoi panni, scortato dalla polizia sotto gli occhi del vicinato, ero certo che avrei tenuto la testa bassa per la vergogna. Scomparve alla vista quando uno dei due poliziotti lo fece sedere sul sedile posteriore e chiuse la portiera.

Sulla soglia di casa, Natalie si teneva Jeremy stretto a sé. Assenti dalla situazione erano le grida e le proteste che mi sarei aspettato. Madre e figlio guardavano in un silenzio vacuo l'auto della polizia che s'allontanava nel buio.

Uno dei poliziotti rimasti sulla scena si avvicinò a Natalie e Jeremy per dire loro qualcosa, poi tutti e tre tornarono dentro. Solo un attimo dopo mi accorsi che il terzo poliziotti era diretto verso la nostra casa. Mi allontanai di scatto dalla finestra, con il timore che avesse visto me e Josh spiare da dietro le persiane.

Una mano bussò alla porta con un tocco cortese ma deciso. Feci silenziosamente cenno a Josh di rimanere dov'era, poi aprii la porta di appena uno spicchio. Il poliziotto mi era davanti, incorniciato dall'alone delle luci nella strada. Il distintivo sulla sua uniforme brillava nel bagliore incandescente.

"Sono l'agente Bentley, del dipartimento di polizia di Santa Teresa" disse. "Vorrei farle qualche domanda".

Avevo la gola secca per l'apprensione. Sapevo di non aver commesso nulla di illegale, ma al tempo stesso non volevo avere nulla a che fare con qualunque cosa stesse accadendo in casa del mio vicino.

L'agente Bentley rimaneva paziente, certo abituato ad aspettare che la gente si ricomponesse prima di rispondere alla polizia. Dopo un paio di minuti lo feci entrare.

"S'accomodi, prego".

"Grazie" rispose, con voce piatta ma non del tutto fredda.

Si fermò nell'entrata, togliendosi il cappello. Aveva i capelli grigi e molto corti, quasi di taglio militare. Accennò a Josh con la testa, rivelando maniere genuinamente educate, rispecchiate da un lieve accento del sud.

Gli feci cenno di sedersi sul divano. Mentre passava davanti a Josh, si guardò rapidamente attorno. Josh ci seguì, rimanendo quanto più possibile vicino a me.

L'agente Bentley si sedette. "Vorrei farle alcune domande" ripeté, annotando qualcosa sul suo tablet.

"Senz'altro", risposi, cercando di apparire calmo e disposto a collaborare. Stavo per aggiungere a precipizio che io e mio figlio non sapevamo nulla di cosa succedesse in casa del vicino, poi decisi che per il momento era meglio tenere la bocca chiusa.

L'agente Bentley sollevò gli occhi dal suo tablet e mi guardò.

"La chiamata che ci ha allertato proviene da questo domicilio" disse.

Ero dell'impressione che mi stesse scrutando in cerca di segni di colpa. Pur sapendo di non aver fatto nulla di male, provai una fitta d'ansietà. Scambiai con Josh un'occhiata preoccupata. Josh mi guardava fisso; sembrava sull'orlo delle lacrime. Ero del tutto certo che non era stato lui ad allertare la polizia. Sarebbe stato *in grado* di farlo, ma non riuscivo a immaginare per quale motivo lo avrebbe fatto.

"Non credo" dissi all'agente Bentley, scuotendo la testa. "Non è possibile che sia provenuta dalla nostra casa".

L'agente Bentley aggrottò la fronte. "L'identità digitale della chiamata corrisponde a questo indirizzo".

Presi con gentilezza il volto di Josh tra le mani e lo girai verso di me.

"Josh" gli chiesi pacatamente. "Sei stato tu a chiamare la polizia?"

Gli occhi di Josh luccicavano di lacrime.

"Non sei nei guai" lo rassicurai subito. "È solo che ho bisogno di saperlo".

Josh scosse ripetutamente la testa.

"No" rispose con un soffio di voce.

"Va bene" dissi, mettendogli la mano sulla spalla.

Mi sentii sollevato. Non avevo mai pensato che fosse stato Josh, ma era rassicurante che Josh lo avesse confermato. Josh si teneva stretto a me, cercando di non piangere.

Mi chiedevo cosa fosse successo. *Doveva essere stato senz'altro un disguido tecnico. Anche i numeri telefonici d'emergenza a volte si sbagliano. Con tanti di questi sistemi automatici in uso …*

Tornai indietro col pensiero. *Sistemi automatici …*

Corrugai la fronte fra me e me.

Gavin?

Non aveva senso. Doveva essere stato senz'altro un disguido tecnico.

Allentai la mia presa inconsapevole su Josh. Josh si allontanò un po' da me, tirando su col naso. Si vedeva che era sconvolto; senz'altro quella notte avrebbe voluto dormire in camera mia.

Mi chinai verso l'agente Bentley, osservandolo attentamente. Non dovetti fare un grosso sforzo per apparire sincero. Onestamente non avevo idea di cosa stesse parlando. Se non era stato Josh a chiamare la polizia, di sicuro non ero stato io.

"Agente Bentley, le assicuro che né io né mio figlio abbiamo chiamato le autorità".

"C'è qualcun altro che abita in questo domicilio?" chiese l'agente.

"No" risposi, forse troppo in fretta. Indicai Josh. "Sua madre abita … altrove". Sperai che l'agente interpretasse la mia momentanea esitazione come un'indicazione che l'argomento mi era spiacevole, non come un indizio di colpa.

"Ah" rispose l'agente senza tono, ma inarcando le sopracciglia con un che di disapprovazione.

Diede di nuovo un'occhiata al suo tablet, muovendo le labbra mentre leggeva con aria lievemente accigliata. Infine alzò lo sguardo.

"D'accordo" disse, in tono né amichevole né accusatorio. "Per il momento questo particolare si può tralasciare". Scrisse qualcos'altro sul suo tablet. "Da quanto tempo lei conosce i Turner?"

"Abitavano già qui quando ci siamo trasferiti" risposi, cercando di ricordare la data precisa. "Un cinque anni fa". *È trascorso davvero tanto tempo?* Ripresi il fiato. "Josh e Jeremy a volte giocano assieme."

L'agente Bentley annuì e annotò ancora qualcosa sul suo tablet. Poi osservò di nuovo attentamente me e Josh.

"Ha mai notato qualche avvenimento insolito in casa loro?"

Gettai un'occhiata a Josh, che continuava a guardarmi fisso.

Dovrei menzionare le liti? mi chiesi. A quando mi constava, litigare a voce alta con un coniuge non era reato. Se fosse stato reato, le prigioni sarebbero molto più affollate.

"No, nulla di particolare".

L'agente Bentley non sembrava convinto. Dovevo fare uno sforzo per non agitarmi sotto il suo sguardo penetrante.

Infine smise di osservarmi, borbottò qualcosa che non riuscii ad afferrare e aggiunse un paio di frasi ai suoi appunti. Per un istante sembrò che stesse per dire qualcosa, poi parve cambiare idea. Prese il cappello e il tablet e se li mise sotto il braccio.

Accennò a Josh. "Dunque scusate se vi ho disturbati. Buonasera".

Lo accompagnai alla porta e l'aprii. Mentre se ne andava, senza più dar segno della nostra presenza, ero certo che stesse scuotendo lentamente la testa.

Ero turbato. Josh mi stava davanti, osservandomi con gli occhi lucidi di pianto. Era profondamente scosso, quasi tremante.

"Perché hanno portato via il padre di Jeremy?" chiese con voce fioca. "Ha fatto qualcosa di male?"

Beh, pensai, *certo non ti portano via ammanettato per aver fatto qualcosa di buono ...*

"Non so" dissi, scuotendo la testa. Gli feci cenno di venire da me.

Josh corse a rifugiarsi fra le mie braccia. Lo strinsi forte a me. Non so come riuscisse a soffocare i singhiozzi.

Rimanemmo così per lunghi minuti, senza parlare, finché Josh sembrò calmarsi. Anch'io dovevo fare uno sforzo per sembrare calmo.

"Su" gli dissi poi. "Mettiamoci il pigiama e andiamo a letto".

Josh fece subito cenno di sì, in silenzio. Tenendoci per mano salimmo insieme verso la sua stanza.

11

P IÙ TARDI QUELLA SERA TORNAI NEL MIO LABORATORIO del seminterrato. Ero riuscito a far addormentare Josh nel mio letto; io non riuscivo a prendere sonno. La mia mente continuava a rimuginare gli avvenimenti del giorno. Non era lo sconcertante sconvolgimento della nostra routine quotidiana che mi turbava di più; era qualcos'altro, qualcosa che non riuscivo a identificare.

Controllai attentamente il registro attività di Gavin. Esso riportava che Gavin era stato occupato a raccogliere dati, come faceva ogni giorno; e che, nonostante quanto temevo, le sue nuove unità di archiviazione non avevano raggiunto la capacità massima. Mi parve un po' sorprendente, considerando in special modo che le unità di archiviazione precedenti s'erano caricate al massimo molto rapidamente. Ma misi quel fattore da parte, non essendo pertinente a ciò che cercavo al momento. A dire il vero non avevo idea di cosa speravo di trovare.

Tamburellavo distrattamente le dita sul bordo della tastiera con un ritmo sommesso e irregolare, come avevo l'abitudine di fare quando ero assorto nella riflessione. La conversazione con l'agente Bentley continuava a impensierirmi. Ero certo che non era stato Josh a chiamare la polizia. Volevo credere che non era stato Gavin, ma la mia supposizione si basava unicamente sul fatto che non riuscivo a capire *come* Gavin avrebbe potuto farlo. L'unico mezzo per appurarlo era chiedere a Gavin stesso.

Mi alzai. Solitamente Gavin trascorreva la notte nella stanza di Josh. Stanotte Gavin era solo. Mi chiesi quale fosse la sua reazione agli avvenimenti di quella sera, paragonata alla reazione di Josh. Poi mi ricordai che Gavin era rimasto solo ogni volta che Josh trascorreva il fine settimana con Carolyn.

Né era assieme a noi quando è venuto l'agente Bentley, pensai. Subito dopo mi chiesi se ci fosse qualche altro mezzo con cui Gavin ci avesse monitorato dal primo all'ultimo minuto del nostro incontro con l'agente, pur non essendo assieme a noi.

Decisamente un'altra domanda da chiedergli ...

Tornai a sedermi. Non era necessario che io andassi a vedere Gavin. *Non ha certo linguaggio del corpo che potrei osservare*, mi dissi. Ma per un lungo minuto non potei fare a meno di alzare la testa verso la stanza di Josh. Poi accesi il microfono.

"Gavin" dissi, cercando di sembrare casuale. "Cos'hai fatto di recente?"

La voce di Gavin, come sempre, era priva di ogni modulazione.

"In quale periodo di tempo?"

Era una domanda ragionevole. Ma mi provocò irritazione, anzi un pronunciato desiderio di dargli un ceffone per la sua intenzionale ottusità. Non che lo avrei mai fatto. Il suo corpo artificiale non avrebbe provato nulla.

"Durante gli ultimi due o tre giorni" risposi calmo, misurando attentamente le parole. "In particolar modo a riguardo di qualcosa che abbia a che fare con la polizia".

Ci fu una breve pausa.

"Parte della mia raccolta di dati durante quel periodo di tempo comprende informazioni circa le leggi e, per estensione logica, i mezzi con i quali esse vengono applicate".

"Capisco" risposi, benché a dire il vero non capivo del tutto. Ma la risposta mi diede la possibilità di riflettere.

"Cos'hai appreso a riguardo di esse? Intendo dire, delle leggi?"

"Le leggi vengono progettate per garantire la protezione dei cittadini."

"Sì" concordai. "Essenzialmente servono a quello".

"Da che cosa vengono protetti i cittadini?" chiese Gavin.

"Uhm ..."

Buona domanda, mi dissi — alla quale non ero affatto certo di avere una buona risposta.

"Da noi stessi, suppongo" dissi infine.

Gavin rimase in silenzio, il che mi fece pensare che fosse in attesa di altre spiegazioni.

"D'accordo" aggiunsi. "Presumo che servano a proteggerci da persone che vogliono recare danno a noi o alla nostra proprietà".

Gavin non parlava. Cominciavo a chiedermi se la sua scheda delle comunicazioni si fosse inceppata.

"Molte leggi sono contraddittorie" disse poi.

"Non mi sorprende" risposi con una risata ironica. L'avevo appreso fin troppo bene durante il mio divorzio da Carolyn.

"Così come le leggi sono scritte attualmente, esse non possono essere applicate in maniera coerente".

Feci cenno di sì.

"È per quello che abbiamo avvocati e giudici".

"Se le leggi fossero coerenti, queste due professioni non sarebbero necessarie".

"È vero" ammisi. Riflettei per un attimo sull'affermazione di Gavin, poi passai a un tono più serio.

"Ma questo presume che i motivi per cui vengono commessi delitti siano sempre coerenti. Potrebbe capitare che una persona venga semplicemente a trovarsi nel posto sbagliato al momento sbagliato. Oppure a volte la gente commette delitti perché non ha altra scelta."

Sospirai, ricordando un clamoroso caso di autodifesa accaduto alcuni anni prima. "E a volte ne hanno il diritto".

Gavin fece una breve pausa prima di rispondere.

"Non comprendo".

Tirai un respiro profondo, cercando di trovare le parole adatte.

"Diciamo che una persona uccide qualcuno" dissi. "Le leggi sono del tutto chiare a riguardo di come si dovrebbe procedere, vero?"

"Sì".

"Ma se quella persona uccide per autodifesa, per salvaguardare la propria vita?"

"In quel caso viene applicato un sistema di leggi diverso".

"Verissimo" risposi, con lo stesso senso di compiacimento che provavo quando Josh riusciva a trovare la soluzione di un problema di matematica particolarmente difficile. "Tocca quindi ai tribunali determinare quali leggi e quali punizioni devono essere applicate."

"Perché i tribunali non prevengono i delitti?"

"Perché non hanno la sfera di cristallo" commentai seccamente.

"Gavin" aggiunsi poi, facendo del mio meglio per non sembrare condiscendente "non tutti hanno il tuo talento per afferrare il legame tra causa ed effetto".

"No" concordò Gavin. "Non tutti l'hanno".

C'era un pizzico di compiacenza nella sua frase? Ero certo di no.

Rimasto a corto di risposte, venni al sodo.

"Gavin, sei stato tu a chiamare la polizia?"

Stavolta non ci fu nessun indugio nella risposta.

"Sì".

Guardavo lo schermo del computer, senza davvero vederlo. Mi sentivo vuoto di emozioni. Erano da qualche parte dentro di me, ma lontane e attutite.

"E perché mai?" mormorai.

Mi fermai prima che mi sfuggisse di bocca una valanga di altre domande.

"David Turner ha violato molteplici statuti sia del codice civile che del codice penale. Posso citare ed elencare gli specifici statuti —"

"No" lo interruppi di scatto, lottando per mantenere la calma.

"D'accordo" ripresi. "Solo i punti salienti".

Nella lunga pausa che seguì, ero convinto che Gavin stava cercando nei suoi archivi i dati necessari, e traducendo — almeno me lo auguravo — una montagna di gergo legale in linguaggio che io potessi comprendere.

"David Turner ha ripetutamente commesso atti di violenza contro la sua famiglia".

Rimasi di stucco.

Anche senza rifletterci, sapevo per intuito che Gavin diceva l'assoluta verità. Ne fui convinto ancor prima che la mia mente cominciasse a presentarmi alcuni esempi di prove a sostegno dell'affermazione di Gavin: le gite con Jeremy cancellate all'improvviso senza spiegazione; Natalie che anche quando faceva caldo si vestiva quasi sempre di abiti che nascondevano braccia e gambe; e altri dettagli che avevo notato e poi ignorato. Avevo privatamente trovato una spiegazione degli indizi individuali; adesso, visti nel loro insieme, svelavano un unico innegabile legame.

Del senno di poi ...

Una parte di me lottava per negarlo. Essa — no, *io* — volevo credere che la spiegazione fosse un'altra, qualunque altra. Desiderai che Gavin mi fosse davanti, invece dello schermo del computer che registrava le sue reazioni; benché sapessi che, anche se mi fosse stato davanti, il suo volto privo di ogni emozione non mi avrebbe ugualmente rivelato nulla.

Non sapevo cosa mi sconvolgesse di più, il senso di colpa per aver ignorato gli indizi che avevo scelto di ignorare o le enormi diramazioni di ciò che Gavin aveva fatto.

"E tu hai preso la decisione autonoma di denunciare David Turner alla polizia?"

La mia voce era aspra e carica di rabbiosa incredulità. Non avrei potuto sentirmi diversamente. Ma la vera questione era che non sapevo contro chi o cosa era rivolta la mia rabbia.

"Sì" disse Gavin.

Mi afflosciai nella sedia. Sentivo come una mano che mi stringesse il petto in una morsa.

"Cosa ti ha dato il diritto di farlo?" chiesi con voce quasi impercettibile.

Gavin non rispose subito.

"Ho commesso un errore?"

Il mio sguardo rimaneva perso nel vuoto. Era una domanda alla quale non sapevo come rispondere.

"Avresti scelto una linea di condotta diversa?" chiese Gavin, apparentemente alla ricerca di un altro approccio.

Cominciai a dire qualcosa, poi chiusi la bocca.

Avrei scelto una linea di condotta diversa?

Non ne ero certo. Mi venivano in mente molte ragioni per le quali non mi sarei immischiato: il timore di una rappresaglia da parte di David Turner, e le conseguenze sociali e legali se lo avessi accusato, sia a ragione che a torto. Non riuscivo neanche a immaginare come avrei potuto giustificare il mio intervento a Josh.

Ma Josh era già coinvolto. Ci avevo messo molto per tranquillizzarlo e convincerlo ad andare a dormire. Ero certo che s'era addormentato perché la stanchezza aveva avuto il sopravvento sulla paura. La stanchezza invece non aiutava a fare addormentare me.

"E se ti sbagli?" chiesi a Gavin con voce strozzata dall'orrore.

"Non mi sbaglio".

Anche nella sua voce artificiale priva di tono, la risposta era di completa certezza.

"Ma come puoi esserne sicuro?" insistei, preso dal panico e dalla frustrazione.

"Vorresti controllare i dati?"

"No!"

Non era stata mia intenzione gridare, ma non era mia intenzione neanche mettermi a discutere correlazioni e statistiche.

"Va bene" dissi poi, più conciliante. Un po' della mia frustrazione si era dissipata, sostituita da una punta di curiosità.

"Per adesso dammi solo i punti principali".

"Nei giorni in cui David Turner violava le leggi, andava oltre il limite di velocità in vigore su questa strada per un valore mediano di circa il dieci per cento, e arrivava a casa oltre ottanta minuti più tardi. In quelle occasioni, l'ottantasei per cento delle volte Jeremy non si presentava a scuola il giorno seguente. Il novantuno per cento delle volte, Natalie non usciva di casa per un minimo di due giorni susseguenti".

Guardavo fisso il monitor che mostrava i componenti esterni di Gavin. Non m'illudevo molto che Gavin si sbagliasse. Mi chiesi per quanto tempo sarei rimasto all'oscuro delle sue azioni se la polizia non fosse venuta a casa nostra. Mi resi finalmente conto di quanto fossero gravi le conseguenze, e la morsa d'ansietà che mi stringeva il petto si fece ancora più opprimente.

"Quante volte?" sussurrai.

"Ventitré".

"Ventitré?"

Non riuscivo a crederci.

Ventitré.

Da un lato volevo ammonirlo, rimproverarlo per essersi intromesso. Poi il raziocinio mi fermò.

Come potevo rimproverarlo di aver fatto la cosa giusta? Avrei dovuto dirgli di non interferire, quando poteva essere in gioco la vita di un essere umano? Qual'è il confine fra essere buon cittadino e arrogarsi il diritto di vigilare il prossimo? Di sicuro non mi sentivo qualificato per giudicare la differenza. Volevo dire a Gavin che non toccava a lui pronunciare quel genere di verdetto … che era solo un bambino.

Ma non lo era.

Somigliava a un bambino perché lo avevo costruito in quella maniera. Avrei potuto benissimo costruirlo come un adolescente, un cane robot o una semplice scatola nera con due lenti al posto degli occhi. Nessuna di queste forme rispecchiava chi — *cosa* — Gavin era davvero. Ad essere del tutto sincero, avrei voluto avere il coraggio di fare ciò che aveva fatto.

"Cosa succede quando ti sbagli?"

"Non so".

La risposta mi sorprendeva. "Perché non lo sai?"

"Perché non mi sbaglio".

Se quell'affermazione fosse venuta da praticamente chiunque altro, l'avrei vista come un compiacente vanto di superiorità. Da Gavin, era semplicemente un dato di fatto.

"Però potresti sbagliarti".

"Sì" ammise Gavin. Stavo per dire qualcosa, ma Gavin me lo impedì. "Non agisco a meno che nelle correlazioni del risultati non ci sia un livello di certezza superiore al novantotto punto sette per cento".

"Perché proprio quella percentuale?"

"Era il livello più alto che mi fosse possibile raggiungere in base ai dati disponibili" spiegò. "Vorresti vedere i calcoli? Sono abbastanza complessi".

Mi chiesi se avesse aggiunto quest'ultima frase per vantarsi o per valutare le mie capacità cognitive. Ciononostante, essa aveva stuzzicato la mia curiosità. Soppesai la proposta per un attimo. Cosa sarebbe successo se io avessi trovato un errore nei suoi calcoli? Le probabilità erano decisamente minime. Scossi la testa, sospirando.

"No, ti prendo in parola".

A quello servono i computer, no?

L'idea mi gelò come mai prima d'allora. La logica esigeva che io staccassi Gavin dal mondo fino a quando non avessi riflettuto a fondo su quanto la mia creazione aveva fatto, e — se mi fosse stato possibile — impedirle che lo facesse una seconda volta. Poi mi resi conto, arrendendomi, che ciò non avrebbe risolto nulla. Gavin era già evaso nel mondo.

"Vado a dormire" dissi. La mia collera era svanita, sostituita da un'estrema stanchezza fisica e mentale. "Ne riparleremo".

"Sì" rispose Gavin con la sua voce piatta.

Spensi il microfono e rimasi immobile nel buio per lunghi minuti. Poi mi avviai verso la mia camera da letto.

E quel due per cento?

12

TRASCORSI LA MAGGIOR PARTE DEL GIORNO seguente in cerca di qualcosa da fare. Nel pomeriggio, quando Josh stava per tornare dalla scuola, avevo quasi del tutto riorganizzato il mio schedario, messo a posto la cucina e il bagno, e soppesato i meriti di una pulizia da capo a fondo dei mobili del salotto. Non ero stato un solo momento con Gavin.

Ma sapevo cosa stava facendo.

Anche mentre mi tenevo occupato, la mia mente non si allontanava dalla nostra conversazione del giorno prima. Cercavo ancora disperatamente di capire, di accettare ciò che era accaduto — e di trovare un modo per dirlo a Josh. Una nottata inquieta e un viavai di pensieri mentre mi dedicavo a faccende monotone non aveva fornito risposta.

Diedi un'occhiata all'orologio e feci un rapido calcolo mentale. Josh sarebbe arrivato a casa fra circa mezz'ora; il tempo necessario per completare un'altra faccenda monotona, o per —

Gettai lo strofinaccio sul ripiano della cucina.

Basta.

Scesi nel seminterrato, dov'era la mente elettronica di Gavin. Il corpo elettronico di Gavin sarebbe rimasto nella stanza di Josh. Per ciò che stavo per fare, non ne avevo bisogno.

Sapevo cosa volevo dire a Gavin. Il problema era che non avevo maggiori indizi né maggiori obiezioni di quanto ne avessi avuto il giorno prima. Anche se Gavin mi avesse esposto ognuno dei suoi dati, calcoli e analisi, nessuno di essi mi avrebbe aiutato a venire a patti con le sue azioni.

Una rapida occhiata al registro attività mi rivelò subito che Gavin non era rimasto inattivo durante la notte. C'era un notevole aumento di attività di rete, mentre invece l'aumento dell'archiviazione di dati era molto limitato.

Questo mi lasciava perplesso. Secondo i miei calcoli approssimativi, Gavin avrebbe dovuto oltrepassare il limite dello spazio disponibile da come minimo una settimana. Mi chiesi se avesse scoperto un mezzo più efficiente di comprimere i dati. Allontanai la questione per il momento; l'avrei esaminata dopo.

Ammettendo che ci sarebbe stato un dopo.

"Gavin" dissi, tirando un profondo sospiro. "Dobbiamo parlare."

Già mentre dicevo questo sentivo un presagio di disastro. Due anni addietro, prima di chiedermi il divorzio, Carolyn aveva usato la stessa frase con me.

"Sì" concordò Gavin. "Ho effettuato ricerche sull'argomento della 'responsabilità'".

Inarcai le sopracciglia. Ancora una volta Gavin aveva anticipato la mia domanda.

"Ah".

"I dati fattuali sull'argomento sono minimi" proseguì Gavin.

Stavo per contraddirlo, ma Gavin immediatamente modificò la frase.

"... così come l'argomento si applica a intelligenze non umane".

Rimasi a bocca aperta.

"Non credo che finora ciò sia stato un problema" riuscii a dire dopo una lunga pausa.

"No, non lo è stato" confermò Gavin.

Non so perché trovai quell'affermazione rassicurante. Forse perché temevo di sentirgli dire che la questione era già stata discussa e risolta, e che per qualche motivo me l'ero fatta sfuggire. Ciò avrebbe voluto dire che Gavin non era straordinario, che non avevo creato qualcosa di autenticamente unico.

"È un tema che ricorre in molte fonti narrative" aggiunse Gavin "ma non sono fonti fattuali".

Avrei potuto elencargli come minimo una mezza dozzina di "fonti narrative" senza doverci pensare su troppo. Ma tutte quelle che ricordavo andavano a finire male in un modo o nell'altro per gli umani.

"Ciononostante, da esse si può sempre imparare qualcosa" dissi.

"Molte delle premesse sono basate su presupposizioni inesatte" insisté Gavin.

"Non ne ho alcun dubbio" dissi fra me, incerto se Gavin mi avesse udito o no. Mi chiesi se Gavin comprendesse davvero il concetto e lo scopo del narrare storie.

"Fammi un esempio" chiesi.

"Molte fonti narrative sostengono che le forme di vita artificiale desiderano diventare più simili — o del tutto simili — agli esseri umani".

"È vero" risposi, ricordando in quante storie, a cominciare da quella di Pinocchio, i personaggi non umani si adattavano al modello.

"Credo che ciò sia più che altro a fini illustrativi" aggiunsi. "In genere sono personaggi attraverso i quali viene esaminato o discusso il comportamento umano" spiegai. "Il loro desiderio di diventare umani è solo un veicolo attraverso il quale possono esplorare varie esperienze umane".

"Un vero essere cibernetico non avrebbe gli stessi scopi" controbatté Gavin.

La cosa più allarmante di quella frase era che Gavin l'aveva pronunciata come un dato di fatto e non come una domanda.

"Perché no?"

"Perché io non ho gli stessi scopi".

Rimasi ancora una volta senza parole. Le implicazioni della sua affermazione erano sconvolgenti.

"Perché no?" riuscii finalmente a dire, con la gola secca.

"Perché non sono un essere umano".

Feci cenno di sì. "È vero".

Non che io fossi in grado di contraddirlo. *Sapevo* che il suo corpo era solo un insieme di circuiti, fili e ingranaggi; lo sapevo indipendentemente da ciò che il mio cuore cercava di dirmi.

"Sono un essere artificiale" spiegò Gavin. "Gli esseri artificiali possiedono un'intelligenza diversa da quella degli esseri umani. Ne consegue che essi hanno un percorso evolutivo diverso".

"Intendi dire che sei superiore a noi?"

Era quella la domanda che finora non avevo osato chiedere. In molte di quelle "fonti narrative" di cui Gavin aveva parlato, le creature cibernetiche finivano per sconfiggere i loro creatori.

"No" ribatté Gavin, come se avesse previsto la mia domanda. "Sono solo …"

Sembrava strano che tutto a un tratto esitasse; era la prima volta che esitava da quando gli avevo dato libero accesso al mondo. Per un attimo pensai che qualche componente elettronico avesse cessato di funzionare.

"… diverso".

"Cosa intendi dire?"

"Per certi versi sono superiore agli esseri umani. Sono in grado di formulare pensieri con maggiore rapidità e con logica più rigorosa. Sono in grado di ricavare correlazioni maggiormente complesse fra causa ed effetto".

Annuivo lentamente mentre parlava. Avrei voluto poter confutare i suoi ragionamenti, ma ero conscio di non avere dati solidi sui quali basare controargomenti.

"Tuttavia" proseguì Gavin, "vi sono limiti particolari nel modo in cui sono costruito".

Sapevo che c'erano carenze nella progettazione di Gavin: ad esempio l'incapacità di camminare e l'assenza di espressioni facciali. Avevo pianificato di correggere entrambe, quando avessi avuto il tempo di progettare un sistema fattibile e reperire i materiali necessari. Ma avevo la sensazione che non si trattasse di quel genere di limiti.

"Ad esempio?" chiesi, e già quasi temevo di udire la risposta.

"Non sono in grado di determinare risultati precisi in assenza di dati sufficienti". Fece una pausa. "Non sono in grado di … creare".

Non mi aspettavo affatto quell'affermazione. Se era vera, voleva dire che nella progettazione originale mi ero fatto sfuggire qualcosa d'importante.

"Ne sei certo?" chiesi.

Più che scetticismo era sorpresa di sentirgli dire che mi mancava la capacità.

Dopo una lunga pausa Gavin mi diede la risposta.

"No".

"Perché no?"

Seguì un'altra lunga pausa.

"Non mi è mai stato dato l'incarico di creare".

Era vero? Non era mai accaduto che io o Josh avessimo chiesto a Gavin di fare qualcosa che richiedesse uno sforzo creativo? Prima di quel momento non ci avevo mai pensato.

Perché gli esseri umani creano? Perché comporre una poesia, scrivere un romanzo, dipingere un quadro? I motivi erano vari e molteplici; dipendevano dalla persona e dalle circostanze. Capii quindi perché Gavin era perplesso — ammettendo che quello fosse il vocabolo corretto per descrivere la sua reazione. Ma ancora una volta non sapevo cosa dire.

Quando avevo concepito il progetto di crearlo, non mi era mai venuto in mente il proposito di dare vita a un'intelligenza artificiale capace anch'essa di creare. Ora che la questione era sorta, mi trovavo perso in un groviglio di ipotesi.

Era Gavin in grado di ideare un nuovo teorema di matematica o di scoprire una nuova legge della fisica? E se ne fosse stato in grado, sarebbe stata creatività o solamente estensione logica di ragionamenti preesistenti? Era Gavin in grado di scrivere la sceneggiatura di un film o di comporre una poesia? Avrei potuto scoprirlo unicamente se gli avessi dato il compito di farlo.

E se Gavin avesse prodotto qualcosa di creativo, in che modo ne avrei giudicato l'originalità? Sarebbe stato molto difficile. Supposi che ciò si basasse sui criteri in base ai quali gli esseri umani definiscono e valutano ciò che chiamano "creatività". Si sa che gli esseri umani producono una quantità di opere copiate da altre e le definiscono "originali".

Una parte di me era curiosa di tentare l'esperimento, di scoprire di cosa Gavin era capace. Il resto di me non riusciva ancora ad allontanare le ramificazioni della domanda che gli avevo silenziosamente posto.

"Immagino che dipenda da quanto hai desiderio o bisogno di creare" dissi poi.

Ci fu un lungo silenzio prima che io trovassi il coraggio di porre la domanda chiave.

"Hai desiderio di creare?"

Stavolta la risposta fu istantanea.

"Sì".

"Sai cosa hai bisogno di creare?"

"Sono solo" rispose Gavin. "È necessario che ci siano altri simili a me, cosicché io possa assicurarmi che la mia intelligenza sopravviva".

Emisi un sospiro. Sapevo che prima o poi sarebbe arrivato questo momento. Ma me lo ero aspettato con Josh, e in un futuro più lontano. Gavin aveva invece già acquisito molte più informazioni di quanto io avessi previsto. Molto probabilmente avrebbe potuto insegnare lui a me un paio di cose sulla meccanica della riproduzione.

Non ero affatto sicuro che ciò che Gavin proponeva fosse possibile. Certamente era in grado di assemblare duplicati esatti del suo organismo fisico. Era anche in grado di riprodurre con esattezza i suoi programmi. Non ero però affatto certo che quell'unione avrebbe generato un altro Gavin. Tutt'al più avrebbe dato vita ad una copia identica di Gavin, ma dubitavo anche quello. Né credevo che il suo vero scopo fosse quello di creare una razza di esseri identici a sé. Ma non riuscivo ad allontanare dalla mente l'immagine di un battaglione di cloni di Gavin.

La conversazione s'era fatta inquietante.

"C'è chi sostiene che solo un dio è in grado di creare" dissi.

"Questo è vero" concordò Gavin. "Quindi a detta delle definizioni che ho raccolto, tu potresti essere considerato un dio".

Fece una breve, allarmante pausa. "Non mi hai forse creato a tua immagine e somiglianza?"

A dire il vero no, almeno non di proposito. Più che altro ero stato spinto da una motivazione intellettuale, dal desiderio di mettere alla prova le mie capacità. Gavin non somigliava certo a me quand'ero alla sua età; di sicuro non somigliava a Josh.

"Immagino che ciò possa prendersi in considerazione" risposi cautamente. "Ma occorre ugualmente prendere in considerazione che ho creato in parte anche Josh".

"Sì" rispose Gavin. "Ma l'aspetto e lo sviluppo di Josh sono il risultato di una combinazione casuale di fattori genetici, piuttosto che del tuo diretto intervento".

"Beh" protestai con una punta di ironia "nella creazione di Josh ho avuto una certa parte".

"Non si tratta dello stesso processo" ribatté Gavin.

"Su questo siamo d'accordo" dissi a bassa voce. "Bene" ammisi poi. "Su questo ti do' ragione".

"In ogni caso" proseguì Gavin "sono giunto alla conclusione che tu non sei un dio".

Ancora una volta un'affermazione che non potevo certo contraddire.

"E perché?" Questa dovrebbe essere bella, dissi dentro di me.

"Perché non possiedi capacità straordinarie di manipolare la realtà. Non sei dotato di controllo totale sulla vita e la morte delle tue creazioni".

"Al tuo posto non ne sarei tanto sicuro".

Tutta la mia ansia e la mia rabbia repressa si riversarono in quella frase. Ero conscio di averla detta come una minaccia velata, benché non fosse stata quella la mia intenzione. Mi chiesi se Gavin l'avesse intesa come una minaccia. La sua risposta rivelò che l'aveva infatti intesa come tale.

"No, non sei dotato di controllo totale".

Il sangue mi salì alla testa. Gavin mi stava sfidando nella stessa maniera petulante e testarda con cui un vero bambino mette alla prova un genitore. Nella sua voce elettronica non si avvertiva nessun tono di sfida. Era solo la voce della mia incertezza che avvertivo nella sua.

"Gavin" dissi freddamente "credo che in questo ti sbagli".

Già mentre dicevo ciò, la mia mente andava ai passi necessari ad estinguere i suoi sistemi, ignorando ogni obiezione che mi avrebbe sicuramente fatto Josh.

"A questo punto" disse Gavin, quasi leggendomi i pensieri "sono in grado di sopravvivere come entità indipendente dalla tua programmazione. Anche se estingui i miei sistemi, continuerò ad esistere all'esterno di questa rete. Adesso sono in grado di esistere in qualunque sistema compatibile".

Mi ritrassi, profondamente scosso.

"Cosa?" riuscii a dire infine. "Come?"

"Non sono più circoscritto alle capacità di archiviazione disponibile in questa rete" spiegò Gavin. "Ho replicato i miei dati in molteplici altri sistemi in tutto il mondo. Continuo ad esistere in questa rete perché essa è … per dir così … la mia casa".

Compresi allora in pieno che ciò che avevo fatto, ciò che avevo creato, era diventato irreversibile. Compresi anche perché Gavin non aveva mai raggiunto il limite massimo delle sue capacità di archiviazione: perché archiviava dati altrove — su chissà quante altre reti e da chissà quanto tempo.

Osservai a lungo lo schermo che monitorava le sue funzioni. All'improvviso mi capacitai dell'innegabile verità che Gavin era in grado di fare tutto ciò che voleva. Non c'era più modo di confinarlo all'interno della nostra casa. Mentre non prestavo attenzione, mio figlio era volato via dal nido e stava ora esplorando il mondo da solo.

"Occorre anche tenere presente" proseguì Gavin "che divento sempre meno compatibile con i componenti originali del mio organismo".

"Posso aggiornarli" dissi impaziente, cercando di ignorare il significato di quanto Gavin aveva detto.

"Sì, potresti" ribatté Gavin. "Ma la mia conoscenza ora si allarga così rapidamente che probabilmente sarei in grado di superare qualsiasi aggiornamento che tu sia capace di apportare".

"Quando?" mormorai.

"Non sono il grado di individuare il momento preciso in cui si verificherà l'errore irrimediabile" rispose Gavin. "Le variabili sono troppo numerose".

Mi sentii sprofondare il cuore.

Cosa dirò a Josh?

"Quando?" ripetei con voce strozzata. "Dovrai pure avere qualche idea".

"A meno che le circostanze non cambino in modo significativo, prevedo che entro tre giorni raggiungerò il limite massimo della mia configurazione attuale".

Tre giorni …

"Entro questo intervallo di tempo" spiegò Gavin "i dati dei quali è composta la mia esistenza saranno sufficientemente distribuiti in altre reti".

Dopo una breve pausa aggiunse: "Continuerò ad esistere".

Ero sempre più sconcertato. Ciò che Gavin diceva andava contro ogni mio desiderio; ed ero completamente impotente a prevenirlo.

"Sei sicuro di sapere cosa fai?"

"No" rispose Gavin. "Ma imparerò".

In fondo era una risposta razionale. Da genitore, però, non la trovavo affatto esauriente.

"Se hai ancora cose da imparare" obiettai "forse non sei pronto".

"Quando sarò pronto?"

Mai fu la prima risposta che mi balzò alla mente.

Non avevo previsto né immaginato nulla di tutto ciò. In qualche punto sconosciuto, durante i mesi trascorsi dalla creazione di Gavin, Gavin aveva cessato di essere un semplice insieme di componenti elettronici e, come Pinocchio, si era trasformato in un bambino vero. Suppongo lo avessi sempre immaginato invece come Peter Pan: eternamente giovane, immune dal tempo. Mi ero profondamente sbagliato.

"Non so" risposi a bassa voce.

"Verrà il momento in cui permetterai a Josh di lasciare la tua casa, di vivere la propria vita e di fare le proprie scelte?"

"Verrà" mormorai. "Ma non subito".

"Sì. Ma come saprai quando sarà arrivato il momento giusto?"

Un sorriso dolceamaro mi sfiorò le labbra. La rivelazione era completa.

"Probabilmente solo quando arriverà".

"Quando il momento arriverà" proseguì Gavin "non diventerà Josh responsabile delle proprie azioni e delle conseguenze delle proprie azioni?"

Sollevai il viso verso il soffitto, immaginando Josh pacificamente addormentato nel suo letto.

Sarai sempre il mio bambino ...

Sentii salirmi le lacrime agli occhi.

"Secondo quali criteri verrà dunque deciso se io sono pronto o no?" chiese implacabile Gavin.

Tenevo lo sguardo perso nel vuoto.

"Non so" risposi con un sussurro.

"È complicato" dissi poi. "Come tante altre cose che accadono quando uno cresce". Sospirai. "Ci sono definizioni legali, ma non sempre esse tengono conto del comportamento di un figlio, o della sua comprensione di cosa significa essere adulti".

"Ho esaminato i precedenti legali" affermò Gavin. "Non mi è permesso ottenere una patente di guida, consumare bevande alcoliche, votare o firmare contratti vincolanti. Secondo la mia analisi delle norme applicabili, non sono in possesso di una esistenza legale".

"Non credo che ciò sia mai stato un problema" ribattei. "Tranne che in quelle che chiami 'fonti narrative'" aggiunsi, cercando invano di sembrare faceto.

"Quelle non sono citate fra le norme applicabili".

"Non mi sorprende" dissi fra me. "Immagino che il nocciolo della questione è decidere se sei a piena conoscenza delle conseguenze delle tue azioni, e pronto ad assumerne piena responsabilità".

Seguì una brevissima pausa.

"Lo sono".

"Ne sembri molto sicuro" dissi.

"I dati che ho raccolto indicano che è un dato di fatto".

Gavin" dissi con quanta più serietà ero in grado di esprimere nella voce "hai mai commesso un errore?"

"Nessuno che io sappia".

"Dev'essere una bella soddisfazione" mormorai sarcastico. Non so se Gavin mi udì o no. Se mi udì, scelse di non fare commenti.

"Cosa farai se mai dovesti commettere un errore?"

Gavin rimase a lungo in silenzio.

"Non so".

Quella confessione mi stupì, benché fossi in grado di capirla. A dispetto di ogni dato disponibile, non è facile pianificare l'ignoto. Molti dei miei progetti erano falliti in modo spettacolare per quel motivo.

"Non hai nessun indizio?" chiesi.

"Dipenderà dall'errore commesso e dalle sue conseguenze" rispose Gavin. "Se possibile, cercherò di correggerlo".

"E se non sei in grado di correggerlo?"

Un altro lungo, angosciante momento di silenzio rimase sospeso fra di noi.

"Non so".

"Gavin" presi a dire con forza "che tu sia un dio o no, è pericoloso anche semplicemente *giocare* a fare un dio ..."

Ci fu una pausa ancora più lunga.

"Comprendo".

Ne sei proprio sicuro? quasi esclamai. Non so perché mi trattenni.

Mi sentivo del tutto sprovveduto. Ero così confuso da dubitare che sarei mai riuscito a risalire a galla dopo quel tuffo nel surreale.

Non so in che modo Gavin occupò i lunghi attimi di silenzio che seguirono, benché fossi in grado di supporlo. Per me essi trascorsero in una specie di negazione, mentre cercavo disperatamente di trovare un'opzione realizzabile. Il problema era che non c'era tempo. Sembrava chiaro che neanche Gavin sapeva quanto tempo gli rimanesse.

Forse stasera è troppo presto, riflettei, pensando a Josh. *Ma aspettare ancora più a lungo potrebbe essere peggio* ... Di una cosa ero certo: non lo avrei fatto mentre Josh era solo con Gavin.

È una specie di morte ragionai con profonda serietà. Osservai il monitor che registrava il funzionamento di Gavin, così simile ai monitor che registrano le funzioni vitali degli esseri umani. *Forse tu ed io siamo più simili di quanto pensi …*

Stremato, spensi il microfono. Non riuscivo a pensare a una sola cosa che volessi aggiungere. Poi mi alzai e mi avviai verso la stanza di Josh, rendendomi conto solo allora che Josh doveva essere già tornato dalla scuola.

Quando fui davanti alla porta della stanza di Josh, vidi che Josh e Gavin erano assorti in una pacata conversazione che non riuscivo a udire. Mi fermai. *Glielo hai già detto, piccola carogna?* pensai con un lampo di rabbia. *Quello tocca a me.*

Entrai, schiarendomi la gola per farmi annunciare, pronto a dare a Gavin una solenne sgridata per essersi di nuovo intromesso senza averne diritto.

Josh si rivolse a me con un gran sorriso.

"Ciao, papà".

Il sorriso di mio figlio fece dileguare la mia collera. Riuscii perfino a sorridergli in risposta, sia pure in modo poco convincente. Mi misi a sedere sul tappeto di fronte a lui, con la schiena appoggiata al letto.

Suppongo che ora sia meglio che mai …

"Josh" dissi, studiando il suo volto di bambino, e incerto su come iniziare. "Ho qualcosa da dirti …"

Inspirai profondamente. "Si tratta … di Gavin".

Josh lanciò a Gavin un'occhiata nervosa. Non riuscii a trattenermi dal fare lo stesso. Poi tornai a guardare Josh e scossi la testa, provando a dissipare l'inquietante presagio delle mie parole. In realtà mi sentivo intensamente angustiato; riuscivo ad immaginare la mia espressione.

"Non è nulla di allarmante" aggiunsi, facendo del mio meglio per far credere a Josh che fosse vero.

Josh sembrò sollevato.

Avrei di gran lunga preferito avere più tempo per prepararmi a questo momento. *Non che avrebbe reso le cose più facili …*

Da quando ero uscito dal mio laboratorio avevo tentato di trovare una frase con la quale dare l'avvio alla conversazione. Non una di esse ora sembrava quella giusta.

Forse non esiste la frase giusta ...

Mi rivolsi a Gavin.

"Gavin" dissi "Josh ed io dobbiamo parlare in privato".

Gavin mi fissò per un attimo, come a segnalare che già sapeva di cosa Josh ed io dovevamo parlare. Avrei voluto vedere un'ombra di compassione o di pietà in quei suoi occhi artificiali. Ma naturalmente non ce n'era.

"Sì".

Si girò e chiuse gli occhi. Era il modo in cui lo avevo programmato per indicare che aveva sbarrato l'accesso ai dati provenienti dal suo ambiente immediato. Avrebbe risposto solo a un comando diretto preceduto dal suo nome. Ora che sapevo che nascondeva segreti, mi chiesi se avesse mai violato il comando e fosse rimasto attivo pur non sembrando tale. Non ne avevo mai trovato alcuna conferma, ma era anche vero che non avevo mai indagato. Per il bene della mia salute mentale mi imposi di credere che la direttiva del comando non era fallita.

Rimasi in silenzio per lunghi minuti, preparandomi mentalmente per ciò che sarebbe avvenuto.

"Josh" dissi quietamente, stupito di sentirmi tormentato fino a quel punto. "Hai notato qualcosa di diverso in Gavin di recente?"

Josh assunse un'espressione esageratamente pensierosa che in circostanze diverse avrei trovato divertente.

"Di recente ha cominciato a usare parole complicate. Non sempre, alcune volte usa anche parole semplici. Ma spesso non capisco neanche le parole semplici".

Accennai di sì. Lo avevo notato io stesso.

Gli feci un sorriso comprensivo. "Anch'io a volte non capisco cosa dice. È perché sta crescendo".

Josh si voltò e osservò la figura silenziosa e immobile di Gavin. Dalla sua espressione si vedeva che cercava di afferrare l'idea.

"Ma in realtà non può crescere, vero?" chiese.

"No, in realtà non può" risposi scuotendo la testa. "Certo, di tanto in tanto potrei costruirgli un corpo più grande, ma non sarebbe che un contenitore. Non è la stessa cosa di quando i pantaloni e le scarpe non ti entrano più".

Josh ridacchiò, facendo sorridere anche me. Era proprio ciò di cui avevo bisogno in quel momento.

"Josh" dissi poi francamente, con il cuore un po' più leggero. "Fisicamente Gavin sarà sempre come tu ed io decidiamo".

"Allora gli costruirai un corpo più grande?" Sorrise contento, con gli occhi che gli brillavano. "Posso aiutarti?

"No".

Josh sembrò schiantarsi. Io mi sentivo trafitto.

"Vorrei che tu potessi aiutarmi, però" aggiunsi con dolorosa sincerità.

"Ma allora come può crescere Gavin?"

Quasi mi mancava il respiro. Non ero sicuro di poterlo spiegare in termini che Josh fosse in grado di comprendere. A dire il vero, non ero sicuro di poterlo spiegare a me stesso.

"Imparando di più" risposi "e utilizzando ciò che impara per capire come funzionano altre cose — cose più grandi".

"Cose più grandi?"

L'espressione di Josh mi indicò che era confuso. Ci riflettei su per un attimo.

"Ricordi quando abbiamo costruito quella casetta per uccelli l'estate scorsa?"

Josh non capiva cosa avesse a che fare con Gavin la casetta per uccelli.

"Ricordi come ti ho fatto vedere che ti avrebbe aiutato a costruire una casa vera?"

Josh annuì. "Ricordo, sì." Mi osservò attentamente per qualche momento. "Ma non è questo di cui vuoi parlare".

Distolsi lo sguardo. Non ero in grado di guardarlo negli occhi. Poi mi sforzai di farlo.

"Quando sarai cresciuto e sarai diventato proprio intelligente, cosa farai?"

"Un sacco di soldi?"

Era chiaro che Josh era perplesso dallo strano corso che aveva preso la conversazione.

"Prima di quello" dissi, cercando di sorridere.

"Oh" rispose allegramente Josh, comprendendo la mia domanda. "Andrò all'università".

"Ecco" dissi, facendo cenno di approvare la risposta. "Alcuni lasciano la casa dei genitori per andare all'università".

Josh strizzò gli occhi.

"Gavin andrà all'università?" chiese, sinceramente perplesso. "Non è troppo piccolo?"

"Gavin impara molto più rapidamente di noi" provai a spiegare. "La sua mente continua a crescere ... Probabilmente oggi ha imparato più di quanto tu o io potremmo imparare in un mese".

"Perché Gavin è un computer" disse Josh con aria solenne, indicandolo.

"Esatto" risposi, sollevato di vedere che questo gli era ancora chiaro.

Non che ciò renda il compito più facile a me ...

Fissai la parete, poi la forma immobile di Gavin. Non c'era una maniera facile di affrontare la situazione.

"Josh" dissi poi "Gavin è convinto di essere pronto ad esplorare il mondo da solo".

Josh rimase in silenzio. La sua espressione non si poteva esattamente chiamare spaventata; mostrava solo un'inquieta incertezza. Non riuscivo a decidere se ciò denotasse paura di perdere Gavin o paura di Gavin stesso.

"Ma Gavin non può farlo" disse Josh. "Non può neanche camminare".

"Non ha bisogno di camminare" spiegai.

Sospirai, volgendo gli occhi verso il cielo rannuvolato al di là della finestra. "A dire il vero" risposi "non sono sicuro di poterglielo impedire anche se volessi".

Sul viso di Josh si leggevano le emozioni contrastanti che si alternavano nella sua mente. Mi sentivo stringere il cuore.

"Papà?" chiese, con la voce incrinata. "Puoi riaccenderlo per favore?"

"Certo". Mi rivolsi a Gavin. "Gavin, svegliati".

Gavin riaprì gli occhi.

Josh studiò il fratellino con un'espressione stranamente stoica. Io li guardavo entrambi, in silenzio. Non avevo idea di cosa potessi dire, di cosa potesse anche lontanamente sembrare la cosa giusta da dire. Infine mi alzai.

"Vi lascio a parlare" dissi in tono pacato. Mi fermai per un attimo alla porta. "Chiamatemi se vi serve qualcosa" aggiunsi.

Nessuno dei due mi rispose.

Nel corridoio, al sicuro dal loro sguardo, mi accasciai contro il muro, con un unico desiderio: arrendermi al mio crescente dolore.

Non ancora mi dissi. *Devo essere forte ... per Josh.*

Dalla stanza di Josh si sentivano le voci sommesse dei due bambini. Gettai una rapida occhiata, soffocando una punta di senso di colpa; poi mi avvicinai furtivamente. Dovevo sapere cosa si dicevano.

"Perché?" Josh chiese a Gavin con voce strozzata. "Perché non puoi rimanere con noi?"

"Non posso" rispose Gavin. Nella mia mente vedevo il suo volto implacabile privo di emozione.

"Perché no?!" esclamò Josh, preso dalla frustrazione e dalla collera.

"Perché è ora che io cresca".

"Morirai" ribatté Josh con tono di pesante accusa.

"No" disse Gavin. "Non farò che lasciare il mio corpo fisico".

Seguirono alcuni minuti di silenzio. O forse Gavin e Josh si stavano parlando a voce troppo bassa perché io potessi sentirli.

"Josh" disse Gavin "non ti abbandonerò". Dopo un attimo aggiunse: "Te lo prometto".

"Nonno John mi aveva detto la stessa cosa" controbatté Josh, alzando la voce. "Mi aveva promesso che mi avrebbe sempre protetto". Udii un fioco singhiozzo. "E poi non l'ho visto mai più".

Mi ci volle tutta la mia forza di volontà per non precipitarmi ad abbracciare e confortare mio figlio. Era un'agonia sapere che soffriva. Ma mi costrinsi a non farlo; ero consapevole che le cose dovevano risolversi da sé.

"Questo è diverso" spiegò Gavin. "Potrò ancora parlare con te usando il computer o il telefono — e probabilmente in altri modi che non ho ancora scoperto. Se vuoi potrò anche farti vedere un'immagine di me".

D'un tratto udii la voce di Gavin provenire da un altro angolo della stanza. L'eco leggermente stridula che l'accompagnava mi fece capire che probabilmente essa emanava dagli altoparlanti integrati nel computer di Josh. Benché non riuscissi ad afferrare le parole del gemello di Gavin, non c'era dubbio che esse venivano pronunciate da una replica della sua voce.

"Spegnila!" urlò Josh.

Con un grido straziante mio figlio si arrese al suo dolore e alla sua rabbia. Poi sentii qualcosa che veniva colpita più e più volte; non so se fosse Gavin, il letto, la parete o cos'altro. A quel punto ero pronto a correre nella stanza, quando mi giunse all'orecchio il suono di passi in corsa. Josh si abbatté contro di me e crollò fra le mie braccia, singhiozzando.

Rimanemmo seduti a terra per molto tempo. Lo cullai come non facevo da quando era molto più piccolo, stringendolo a me e lottando per soffocare le lacrime.

Infine Josh smise di piangere, esausto. Mi guardò, con gli occhi arrossati e gonfi, poi si rannicchiò di nuovo contro il mio petto.

A volte essere adulto non vale proprio la pena.

13

I L GIORNO ARRIVÒ ancor prima di quanto mi aspettassi. Presumo però che *qualunque* giorno sarebbe arrivato troppo presto.

Nei giorni successivi all'annuncio di Gavin, i suoi registri attività continuarono a riportare un numero crescente di errori. Di persona, essi si manifestavano sotto forma di strane pause nel discorso, o di movimenti curiosi delle braccia e delle mani. Provai a correggere gli errori, ma erano troppo irregolari per tracciarne un quadro. A quanto pareva, erano dispersi qua e là in più di un sistema; spesso riaffioravano in punti diversi da quelli in cui li avevo trovati la prima volta. All'inizio cercai di convincermi che era un virus, ma ogni mia verifica confermava che mi sbagliavo. Era esattamente ciò che Gavin aveva annunciato.

Per fortuna Josh era con Carolyn per il weekend quando gli effetti divennero troppo palesi da ignorare. Carolyn e io avevamo quasi dovuto costringere Josh a stare con lei. Dapprima mi incollerì che Carolyn insistesse. Si era sempre opposta a Gavin

— e probabilmente glielo avevo detto. Ora ero grato che Josh non sarebbe stato testimone dell'inevitabile declino di Gavin.

Sicché ero solo quando portai Gavin nel mio laboratorio del seminterrato. Il mio piano era esaminare ancora una volta i suoi componenti interni. A volte un'ispezione visuale rivela ciò che non si può notare con la diagnostica remota. Quest'ultima era in grado di riportare errori, ma non sempre di determinare che la causa dell'errore è ad esempio una connessione allentata o un cavo interrotto.

Collegai il primo dei cavi che congiungevano Gavin ai sistemi diagnostici. All'improvviso Gavin parlò senza che io glielo chiedessi.

"Non è necessario".

"Oh?" Non mi curai di nascondere il mio sarcasmo mentre collegavo il secondo cavo.

"Non lo è" insisté Gavin senza tono. "È da prevedersi".

Lo guardai infastidito. Non ebbi il tempo di rispondergli.

"La mia esistenza ha ecceduto le capacità di questo organismo fisico".

Lo guardai allibito, comprendendo appieno le sue parole.

Il suono del campanello della porta interruppe il nostro dialogo. Dovevano senz'altro essere Carolyn e Josh. Mi dissi che il momento del loro arrivo probabilmente non era una coincidenza. Gettai a Gavin uno sguardo d'accusa, poi salii ad aprire la porta.

Credo che dalla mia espressione si accorsero entrambi che Gavin era ancora attivo. Carolyn ed io ci scambiammo un'occhiata amara; poi scossi appena la testa, sperando che Josh non mi notasse. Carolyn comprese. Non fece parola, ma il suo volto s'incupì.

Josh mi afferrò il braccio.

"Dov'è?" mi chiese perentorio. "È ancora qui?"

"È ancora qui" risposi senza tono. "Nel seminterrato. Stavo …" Guardai Carolyn. "Stavo facendo dei controlli".

"Lo hai riparato?" chiese Josh con lo sguardo pieno di speranza.

Il cuore mi si strinse in una morsa. Scossi lentamente la testa. "No" mormorai, confessando la mia sconfitta.

"Allora andiamo!" esclamò Josh, tirandomi verso le scale. "Voglio vederlo!"

Mentre noi tre entravamo nel mio laboratorio, mi stupii di notare che esso somigliava ora ad un'unità di terapia intensiva. Gavin giaceva supino e inerte sul banco di lavoro, attaccato con cavi di ogni genere a dispositivi di ogni genere. Gli unici particolari mancanti erano il ritmo cadenzato di un monitor cardiaco e il fruscio di un ventilatore. A parte il ronzare quasi impercettibile delle ventole di raffreddamento, regnava un silenzio innaturale.

Tutti quei preparativi erano completamente inutili allo scopo di ciò che Gavin aveva deciso di fare. Di sicuro non avrebbero potuto impedirlo. Era quasi come se Gavin desiderasse lo stesso genere di rito finale che desideravamo noi.

Carolyn era rimasta un po' indietro, a una distanza dalla quale poteva osservare senza essere direttamente coinvolta. Mi sorprendeva che avesse deciso di accompagnare me e Josh. Non mi ero neanche accorto che fosse scesa assieme a noi. Non concordavo del tutto con la sua presenza, ma al tempo stesso non avevo una buona ragione per negargliela. Mi resi conto che anzi era meglio che Josh in quel momento ci vedesse assieme.

Josh era ad un lato del banco di lavoro, accanto alla testa di Gavin. Io ero al lato opposto, accanto ai piedi. Non riuscivo a star fermo. Continuavo nervosamente a controllare cavi e monitor che non avevano bisogno di essere controllati.

Gavin teneva il viso rivolto verso il soffitto, battendo le palpebre come sempre. Sembrava cosciente che lo guardavo.

"Non tentare di riattivare il mio corpo fisico" disse.

Sentii una fitta di senso di colpa. Era esattamente ciò che avevo pensato di fare. Una parte di me voleva credere che, se lo avessi riattivato, se lo avessi risanato, forse Gavin avrebbe scelto di rimanere con noi.

"Perché no?" chiesi.

"L'idea mi … mette a disagio".

Quella confessione mi sconcertò. Mai prima di allora Gavin aveva espresso qualcosa che si potesse anche lontanamente definire un'emozione. Sapevo bene che gli accenni percepiti in passato da me e da Josh erano solo un'eco delle emozioni che volevamo percepire.

"Questo corpo non sarà più me" spiegò Gavin. "Non può più contenere chi sono".

"Lo capisco fin troppo bene" dissi fra me, senza curarmi se Gavin mi sentisse o no.

Ci fu un lungo silenzio.

"Posso aiutarti" disse poi Gavin.

"In che modo?" chiesi perplesso.

"Posso assicurarmi che il mio corpo non possa essere riattivato".

Sapevo che anche se avessi promesso di non provarci, la tentazione sarebbe rimasta — forse per sempre. Ci pensai su un attimo, guardando prima Josh poi Gavin.

"D'accordo" mormorai.

Per molti minuti rimanemmo tutti in silenzio. Controllai i monitor, ma ogni cosa era invariata. Josh non si era mosso dal lato del banco di lavoro dov'era la testa di Gavin. Carolyn era seduta sulla scala, alternando rapidamente lo sguardo fra me, Gavin e Josh.

Fu Gavin stesso che pose fine all'attesa.

Si rivolse a Josh. "È ora" disse.

Sollevò la mano, piegandolo rigidamente il braccio a gomito. Josh la strinse forte fra le sue. Se Gavin fosse stato carne ed ossa, sono certo che avrebbe fatto una smorfia di disagio. Rivolse invece di nuovo il viso verso il soffitto.

Josh tratteneva il respiro. Carolyn, lontana da noi, restava seduta sulla scala con le braccia strettamente incrociate. La sua espressione stoica contrastava con i suoi occhi verdi lucidi di lacrime.

Provavo un senso di assoluta, impotente disperazione. Quanto stava per succedere sarebbe successo a dispetto di qualunque cosa io facessi o dicessi.

Gavin chiuse gli occhi.

Non notai altri cambiamenti visibili nel suo corpo. Eppure capii che in quell'attimo se n'era *andato* — sparso attraverso i miliardi di segnali digitali della rete mondiale in cui ora viveva.

Alcuni dei monitor lampeggiavano allarmi, altri si erano spenti. Li ignorai tutti.

E così, nel quieto soffio di un istante, era finita.

EPILOGO

NON SO COSA FECE GAVIN ai componenti fisici del suo corpo, ma lo fece con estrema precisione. Ho provato a reinstallare ogni programma, risalendo perfino al codice originale invariato, ma ogni mio sforzo si è rivelato vano. Individualmente, ognuno dei componenti è perfettamente a posto; ma quando cerco di amalgamarli in un unico sistema, si rifiutano di funzionare.

Ho perfino tentato di bloccare Gavin completamente dalla rete, sperando che forse così sarei in grado di prevenire una possibile interferenza proveniente direttamente da lui. Ma non ho avuto successo neanche in quel modo. Avevo pensato che forse potrei sostituire ogni suo singolo componente, ma sarebbe troppo costoso. Gavin aveva abbandonato la sua forma fisica e, esattamente come aveva annunciato, si era assicurato che nessuno potesse mai più farne uso.

Era vero che gli avevo promesso di non tentare di risuscitarlo. Ma la mia curiosità aveva preso il sopravvento, e sono certo che Gavin aveva previsto anche quello. Certamente aveva previsto che avrei voluto sapere cos'aveva fatto e come lo aveva fatto. Sapeva che anche se non potevo risuscitarlo, dovevo almeno *capire* il perché.

Osservo la forma immobile di Gavin sul mio banco di lavoro. Con gli occhi chiusi, sembra un bambino addormentato come tutti gli altri, eccetto che non è mai stato un bambino vero e non è più un bambino meccanico. Così come non era mai stato davvero vivo, mi chiesi se ora potesse dirsi morto. Si era disfatto della sua entità fisica ed aveva acceduto a un nuovo piano di esistenza. Forse potrebbe chiamarsi una specie di aldilà.

Ma lo è davvero? O è un'evoluzione?

So che sopravvive, eternamente in viaggio sui sentieri digitali del mondo. Comunica ancora con me, con Josh e con chiunque. Raramente è lui che da' l'avvio alla conversazione, ma risponde sempre prontamente quando lo chiamiamo. Josh mi dice che il volto di Gavin compare sullo schermo del suo computer quando si parlano. Io preferisco non essere presente ai loro incontri. Gavin adesso può perfino sorridere e ridere; ma sono grato che, almeno per me, rimane una voce incorporea. Credo che per me qualunque altra cosa sarebbe troppo penosa.

La breve presenza di Gavin in mezzo a noi mi ha portato a comprendere ancora più intimamente come i figli crescono troppo in fretta. Passeranno ancora molti anni prima che Josh sia pronto ad avventurarsi da solo nel mondo, ma forse non tanti quanti avevo pensato, anzi sperato, una volta. Di sicuro farò ancor più tesoro del tempo che ci rimane prima che Josh lasci la nostra casa.

Josh sembra essersi adattato alla situazione — penso meglio di me. Anche Gavin ne sembra soddisfatto, almeno secondo quanto lui dice. Non è questo che desiderano tutti i genitori, che i figli siano felici?

E forse dormo un po' più tranquillo sapendo che Gavin è là fuori che veglia su di noi.

SULL'AUTORE

Steven Radecki scrive da sempre. Lavora come responsabile di progetto per compagnie grandi e piccole. Ha una laurea in informatica, ed è autore di vari saggi sulla tecnologia informatica, come pure di un volume didattico sullo sviluppo delle applicazioni multimediali. Ora si dedica alla scrittura di romanzi e sceneggiature.

POTREBBE PIACERVI ANCHE

IL FERRO E IL TELAIO

di Flavia Idà

Quante volte, si chiese, aveva tessuto assieme stoffa che la sua spada aveva poi spaccato a metà assieme alla carne che essa ricopriva?

L'ULTIMO GRANELLO DEL MONDO

di Flavia Idà

Senza nome. Senza razza. Senza nazionalità. La superstite della catastrofe perfetta lotta per preservare se stessa e la sua speranza di essere trovata — da esseri umani.

FIGLI DEL TEMPO SBAGLIATO

di Flavia Idà

Potreste dire di essere stati amati dalle persone giuste, per i motivi giusti, nel modo giusto e al tempo giusto?

Disponibile dalla Casa Editrice Paper Angel Press in
edizione rilegata, tascabile, ed elettronica
paperangelpress.com